Jean's Golden Term

BY

ANGELA BRAZIL

Author of "Nesta's New School"
"The Little Green School" &c.

Illustrated by Frank Wiles

BLACKIE & SON LIMITED
LONDON AND GLASGOW

By Angela Brazil

The New School at Scawdale.
The School on the Moor.
The School on the Cliff.
Jill's Jolliest School.
Nesta's New School.
The Little Green School.
St. Catherine's College.
At School with Rachel.
Ruth of St. Ronan's.
Captain Peggie.
Schoolgirl Kitty.
The School in the South.
Monitress Merle.
Loyal to the School.
A Fortunate Term.
A Popular Schoolgirl.
The Princess of the School.
A Harum-Scarum Schoolgirl.
The Head Girl at the Gables.
A Patriotic Schoolgirl.
For the School Colours.
The Madcap of the School.
The Luckiest Girl in the School.
The Jolliest Term on Record.
The New Girl at St. Chad's.
For the Sake of the School.
The School by the Sea.
The Leader of the Lower School.
A Fourth Form Friendship.
The Manor House School.
The Nicest Girl in the School.
The Third Form at Miss Kaye's.
The Fortunes of Philippa.
An Exciting Term.
Jean's Golden Term.
The School at the Turrets.
Joan's Best Chum.
The Angela Brazil Omnibus Book.

Printed in Great Britain by Blackie & Son, Ltd., Glasgow

Contents

BOOK
PRODUCTION
WAR ECONOMY
STANDARD

Illustrations

JEAN'S GOLDEN TERM

CHAPTER I

The Dog Show

Jean Barrett woke at seven o'clock one March morning, and, slipping on her dressing-gown, went to her open window, flung back the outside shutters and stepped on to the small veranda. The bright sun was shining upon a view of palms, pine trees, and yellow mimosa, beyond which sparkled the blue waters of the Mediterranean. The crimson creeper that clothed the front of the little hotel festooned her balcony, and below, in the garden, were blooming carnations, geraniums, tulips, and pansies. She looked at the lovely scene with a sigh of satisfaction, for she was a sun-lover and adored flowers. The uncle and aunt who had adopted her years ago, on the death of her parents, were both artists, and spent much of their time abroad, painting, and at present they were staying in the old town of Monaco, where they found many subjects for their brush.

Jean enjoyed the happy, roving, dilettante life, going from place to place in search of fresh scenes, meeting artists and musicians, and wandering, like the gipsies, to any spot where the beauty of the landscape attracted them. Her education, it is true, had suffered considerably. Her aunt gave her desultory lessons in English subjects, she had picked up a smattering of French and Italian, a Spanish friend had taught her to play the guitar and to sing some songs, and she often went sketching with her uncle. Compared, however, with any other English girl of twelve she would have been pronounced decidedly backward. She had no acquaintance with decimals, her history was hazy, and her geography was acquired by personal knowledge of the places she had visited.

Sometimes Mrs. Barrett directed a half-hearted attention to Jean's deficiencies in this respect, and spoke of sending her to school, but so far her plans had never materialized.

" Why bother? She does very well as she is!" said Mr. Barrett, in his easy, good-natured manner. " Decimals? She can add up accounts in francs and lire, and never lets people give her the wrong·change; so what do decimals matter? I'd miss her if she went away. She helps me to carry my painting traps, and she's always ready to pose as a model when I want to put a figure in a picture. Culture, did you say? Isn't she getting culture by going about the world? I saw a second-hand volume of Shakespeare on a stall in the market yesterday, only five francs, and a good copy in red morocco binding. I'll buy it to-morrow, and she can read it for half an hour every day. Shakespeare ought to give her culture, if anything can."

" Yes, but that isn't quite the same as mixing with girls of her own age," remarked Mrs. Barrett thoughtfully. " I'm afraid she's missing something, and she may reproach us for it when she's older."

" Stuff and nonsense! She's happy enough. Do you want to go to school, piccaninny? Shall we send you to the Lycée here, or the Convent? Which will you choose?"

" Neither, thanks," answered Jean emphatically. " I often see the girls coming out of the Lycée, and I don't like the look of them. As for the Convent, there's an old terror of a Sister Superior there; she marshalls a set of depressed-looking girls to vespers at the cathedral, and pokes them in the ribs from behind if they even move a finger during the sermon. No convent for me!"

" Yet, I rather think——" began Mrs. Barrett.

" Oh, Auntie, please don't think!" interrupted Jean imploringly, " we're so jolly as we are! Uncle Charlie shall buy that copy of Shakespeare—I suppose some English visitor left it behind at Monaco—and I'll read it aloud to him while he paints. I will indeed, and no shirking!"

" I couldn't paint if anybody was reading aloud," remarked Mr. Barrett. " You'll have to get your culture privately, my dear!"

" That's where school comes in," finished Mrs. Barrett.

This conversation had taken place on the previous evening, and this March morning, as Jean, leaning on the flower-festooned railing of her balcony, surveyed the yellow mimosas against the background of the blue sea, she recalled it with a feeling of apprehension. She hoped Aunt Nora was not considering the question seriously. She had no wish to attend the Lycée, a large secondary school in Monaco. The pupils were obliged to be in their classrooms by eight o'clock every morning, and the amount of their home-work seemed to her prodigious. She had watched them pouring out at half-past four with full satchels, and had occasionally spoken to a few of them, looked at their textbooks, which, of course, were in French, and had been appalled at what they were expected to learn during their evening preparation. Jean could converse fairly well in French, but she had little knowledge of its grammar, and the prospect of taking subjects in that language did not appeal to her. She much preferred her easy lessons with Aunt Nora.

Meantime, school was still in abeyance, and she had a day of glorious liberty before her. She left the balcony and dressed quickly. There was a self-imposed task which required her immediate attention. Mrs. Hartley, a fellow guest at the hotel, owned a little Cairn terrier. It slept in her bedroom, and, as she was not an early riser, by mutual arrangement Jean, who adored dogs, tapped at her door at half-past seven each morning, received Barney, and took him for a run before breakfast. It was a delight to both Jean and the dog, who enjoyed a good scamper, and the pair were on terms of intimate friendship.

To-day they went into the public gardens on the cliffs bordering the sea, Jean rejoicing in the beauty of the flowers, and Barney chasing little green lizards, which quickly evaded him by darting into crevices of the walls. They passed the Cathedral, turned down a narrow and picturesque street overhung by archways, and reached the great square in front of the palace of the Prince of Monaco, where they were just in time to watch the changing of the guard, and see the soldiers take their places in front of the red-and-white striped sentry boxes, beside the rows of cannon. Then back through another quaint Italian-looking little street, where women were going about with baskets full of vegetables, to another square, where girls with their satchels were hurrying into the Lycée, and where, from an adjacent convent garden, a tumultuous babel announced that the pupils were still at play, and finally round the corner to the hotel, where delicious hot coffee and rolls and butter were waiting on the table for Jean, and Barney's dog biscuit and dish of water were in their accustomed corner.

Barney's mistress rarely made her appearance downstairs before ten o'clock, but this morning she came into the hotel lounge an hour earlier than usual. She seemed much excited and distraught, and, seeing Mr. and Mrs. Barrett there, at once began to pour out her troubles. She had been wintering in Monaco while her husband travelled on business in Poland and Czechoslovakia. She had just received a telegram to say that he was ill in hospital at Budapest, and that she must go to him at once. She would start by the afternoon train and travel via Genoa and Vienna.

" It will be a very long journey," she explained, " and I shall have to go through so many different countries that I can't possibly take my little dog with me. The customs officers wouldn't allow him to pass. I'd leave him here at the hotel in charge of the concièrge, only I don't want to come back to Monaco. I mean to travel about with my husband in future, in case he should be taken ill again. And what could we do with a dog? He'd only be a nuisance. If you care to have Barney I'll give him to you with pleasure. He likes Jean."

" Oh! Do you really mean it? I'd adore to have him! May I, Uncle?" begged Jean.

" Well, it seems hard on the poor little chap if nobody wants him," said Mr. Barrett. " I think we may offer to adopt him. He'd be a nice companion for you."

" Thank you immensely," said Mrs. Hartley. " You've got me out of a great difficulty. By the by, he's a pedigree dog, and I entered him for the dog show next week at Monte Carlo. I'll give you the papers. You may as well show him. If he wins a prize Jean must take it. I'll write a letter formally bequeathing him to her, then you'll have no trouble with the authorities. I hate to part with him, but I know he'll have a kind mistress. And I can think of nothing but my husband at present. I shall count the minutes till I can get to Budapest. Well! I must go and pack, and I'll give you Barney's papers before I leave. Thank you again for adopting him."

Mrs. Hartley, after a tearful good-bye to her pet, caught the afternoon train, leaving Barney's pedigree, his entrance ticket for the dog show, and a paper, duly witnessed by the manager of the hotel, declaring that he was now the property of Miss Jean Barrett. His new mistress made much of him. She had often longed for a dog of her own, but the opportunity had never come her way before. He was very well trained, and obedient, and so intelligent that he seemed to understand everything she said to him. He was a lively companion for walks, but he would lie down absolutely quietly when she was writing or reading. Even Aunt Nora, who was not particularly fond of dogs, admitted that he was an exception, and began to like him.

The great event to which Jean was now looking forward was the " International Canine Exhibition " that was to take place the next week at Monte Carlo. In preparation for this, Barney underwent much grooming, till his already glossy coat was in the pink of condition. The show was to be held upon the celebrated terrace in front of the Casino, reserved and enclosed that day specially for the purpose. All exhibits must be received before nine o'clock in the morning, so, soon after eight Mr. Barrett and Jean, with Barney on a lead, started off in high spirits. Monaco is only a short distance from Monte Carlo, and half an hour's walk would be a good preparation for what might prove a trying day for her pet. Fortunately the weather was gloriously fine, the Riviera was living up to its reputation, and a clear sky and a calm sea seemed to promise an influx of visitors to the show. They walked through the old town, where the children were already in school, past the palace, and down the steep steps under the ramparts to the harbour, where yachts were anchored and a battleship was moored close to the lighthouse. Here they left picturesque Monaco, with its flower market and its streets planted with orange trees, and mounted up the hill into fashionable Monte Carlo, as different as the reverse side of a coin, with great hotels and handsome shops displaying expensive luxuries for rich purses. The terrace, with the palm trees and beautiful flowers, and its glorious view over the Alpes Maritimes and the Mediterranean, made an ideal setting for the show. Mr. Barrett delivered Barney's papers to an official, and received a ticket with his number. A boy in uniform offered to escort them to the right place, where he must be left, and took them through the entrance gate. Other exhibitors had arrived on the same errand, and they found themselves among a crowd of owners and dogs. The barking was terrific. Some of the exhibits were protesting loudly against their temporary internment; others, on their way to their destinations, showed a tendency to quarrel. Jean caught up Barney in her arms, as a big Alsatian made a snap at him.

"Poor darling! I don't want him to be mauled before he goes to be judged!" she exclaimed. "He'd fight any dog twice his own size, bless him! I hope we haven't to go far. What's his number?"

" No. 29. Here we are. Luckily the small dogs are near the entrance," said Mr. Barrett, as their escort pointed out the corresponding number fixed to a cage.

Long tables had been arranged down the terrace, and on these were placed wired-in pens for the little dogs, and stalls for the larger ones. Barney was fastened into No. 29, supplied with water, and his mistress tried to coax him to endure his prison with patience. After an outburst of indignation, his good training prevailed, and he settled down with submission in his pathetic eyes.

" Let us leave him for a while, and go round the show before there's too big a crush," suggested Mr. Barrett.

" Yes, I want to see the other bow-wows," agreed Jean.

The " Exposition Internationale " had attracted some of the most elect dogs in Europe, and Jean was soon lost in admiration of beautiful exhibits. Choice little Pekinese, reclining on velvet cushions, sniffed scornfully through the wire netting, terriers wagged tails or growled according to their temperaments, a stately Borzoi was being given a final comb by a devoted owner, a magnificent pure white St. Bernard offered Jean a large paw, and an English bulldog greeted her advances with a bored yawn.

After a hurried round of the stalls they returned to Barney, as the judging had already commenced, and his number was an early one. The kennel boy brought Jean a chair, so that she might sit near his cage. The dogs were to be judged in a large wired-in enclosure at the end of the terrace, and presently an official arrived with a ticket bearing the number 29, and told her to come and take her turn.

Releasing Barney from his cage, and carrying him in her arms, she followed the man to the judging court. Here she had to wait while several other Cairn terriers were examined, but at length her number was called, and Barney was admitted into the enclosure. He was a friendly and well-behaved little dog, so submitted quite amiably to being handled by strangers, trotted round the grass plot at his mistress's command, and even licked the judge's hand. A secretary wrote down some notes in French, and Jean was told that the ordeal was over. She carried her pet back to his prison, and gave him a biscuit as a reward for good conduct.

Half an hour afterwards an official appeared with a large pink ticket which he fastened on to Barney's cage.

"Oh! Uncle! Look!" exclaimed Jean. "He's actually won a fourth prize! What luck! I *am* glad!"

"There weren't very many Cairns entered," qualified Mr. Barrett.

"There were ten," said Jean, consulting her catalogue. "So he's better than six of them at any rate. Barney! Do you understand me? You've won a prize! I'm quite sure he knows."

By this time there were many visitors at the show, and ecstatic remarks of admiration for the various exhibits were made in many different European languages. The ladies mostly poured out their enthusiasm over the Pekinese, and the men preferred the sporting dogs. Mrs. Barrett had joined her husband and niece, and was congratulating Jean on Barney's success.

"It's after twelve o'clock," said Mr. Barrett, looking at his watch. "Time to get some lunch, in my opinion. Aren't you hungry, Jean? You hardly ate any breakfast. I vote we leave Barney to himself for an hour, and go to a café."

(E 723)

" Yes, I'm very ready for lunch," agreed Mrs. Barrett. " This barking is deafening, and makes my head ache. I shall be glad to run away from the noise."

" Oh, just five minutes longer," begged Jean. " Barney upset his water. The kennel boy promised to bring him some more, and I want to see that he really gets it. The poor darling is so thirsty. Look at his tongue."

Five minutes is a very short space of time, a tiny interlude in the long years of a life, but those extra five minutes in the show were fateful ones for Jean, and altered her future in a way she could not have anticipated. If she had gone at once, without waiting, what followed might never have happened, and there would have been no story to write about her.

It was Barney who began it all. He wanted his water, he disliked his confinement, and he gave vent to a vehement, impatient bark.

A lady and gentleman who were passing stopped to look at him.

" A nice little Cairn terrier. I see he's won a prize," said the lady.

" So he has," answered the gentleman, then turning he noticed the group standing by the cage, and exclaimed in surprise:

" Hello! Barrett! Who'd have thought of meeting you here? Marjorie, you remember Mr. and Mrs. Barrett and Jean? They were staying last year at St. Tropez."

Mutual greetings and hand shakings followed. Mr. and Mrs. Helm were artists with whom the Barretts had made friends when staying at a small seaside place near Saint Raphael. They had spent happy hours together in one another's studios, had compared pictures, talked art and had said good-bye with reluctance. They had not corresponded, and did not know each other's addresses, so it was by the merest chance that their paths had crossed again.

" We're just going to find a café," said Mrs. Barrett. " Come along with us, and we'll all have lunch together. I want to hear what you've been doing. Did your pictures get into the Salon? Did you send to the exhibition at Rome? Are you staying here? We've been at Monaco all the winter."

As the kennel boy now arrived with Barney's water, and Jean could leave him in comfort, the united party left the show and went to a restaurant in the town. The four artists found much to talk about, and Jean was content to sit and listen to the conversation.

" So you've been at Monaco for several months," said Mrs. Helm at last. " What about Jean? Does she go to a French school here?"

" Well, no," admitted Mrs. Barrett. " We talked of sending her to the Lycée, but she hated the idea of it. She still does lessons with me."

" I carry Uncle Charlie's paint-box, and I'm reading Shakespeare for half an hour every day," said Jean.

Mrs. Helm laughed. She remembered Jean's desultory studies at St. Tropez.

" Why don't you send her to school?" she urged. " How old are you now, Jean? Twelve! You're getting a big girl. It's time you set to work if you're to have any education. Wouldn't you like to go?"

" Not in the least," replied Jean emphatically.

She remembered that Mrs. Helm had raised the question of her education before, when they were at St. Tropez, and it was a subject she wished to avoid. She tried to turn the conversation by speaking of Barney and his prize, but Mr. Helm and Mr. Barrett were talking of future plans.

" I don't think we shall stay much longer at Monaco," said the latter. " I've painted all the best subjects there. And the exchange is so against us that it makes living abroad expensive. We shall probably go back to England soon; in time to send in pictures for the Academy. What are you going to do?"

" We're off to Italy to-morrow. We're only breaking our journey here for a couple of nights. We shall stay in Florence for a while, and then go into the Apennines for the whole of the summer. I want to sketch some of those little hill towns. They're most picturesque. We're trying to let our bungalow in Cornwall for six months or more. By the by, I wonder if it would suit you? It's at Port Erbyn. There's a harbour, and fishing-boats, and some quaint old streets—capital subjects, just the sort you liked at St. Tropez."

" How big is the bungalow?" asked Mrs. Barrett.

" Six rooms *and* a bathroom *and* a larder," replied Mrs. Helm. " You'd find it quite comfortable. There's a very good school for girls, too, at Port Erbyn. We know the two headmistresses. It would be a splendid opportunity for Jean. They have day girls as well as boarders. It's really rather a unique school, run on unusual lines."

Jean, who was eating an ice, and not listening particularly, suddenly became all attention.

" I certainly think it's time we did something with her," said Mrs. Barrett. " I'm afraid she's very much behindhand compared with other girls of her age. She's never done any decimals yet, have you, Jean?"

Jean shook her head gloomily. She began to wish they had not met the Helms.

" She'd soon learn at Tresco House. Each girl gets a large amount of individual attention, which they certainly don't get in a big school where there are often thirty or more in a form. I've some snapshots of the bungalow in my suitcase. I'd like to show them to you. We're staying at ' The Bristol '. Will you come in for coffee to-night, and we could talk things over? We're starting for Italy to-morrow."

" I've often wanted to do some painting in Cornwall," said Mr. Barrett. " I've heard of Port Erbyn. Rather a favourite place for artists, isn't it? Your bungalow might possibly suit us. Yes, we'll come to The Bristol to-night, about nine. As for Jean, I suppose she ought to have a term or two at school. What do you think, piccaninny?"

" I think it's high time I went back to the show to look after Barney," replied Jean, finishing the last spoonful of her ice, and rising from her place at the table.

CHAPTER II

The Mascot

Jean was not included in the invitation to coffee at the Hotel Bristol. She went to bed instead, and from her balcony she watched her uncle and aunt walk away. If Barney had not been in his basket in her room she would have done a little weep. She was full of misgivings for the future. She had so enjoyed the jolly winter at Monaco. She loved the sunshine and gardens and flowers, and their easy happy-go-lucky life there, with its painting and various amusements. She would have been content to stay on and spend the summer in the little principality, in spite of the heat. She knew her uncle had contemplated doing so, and it was annoying that he had suddenly been influenced to alter his plans and to return to England. The prospect of a school of any description did not attract her. She hoped the bungalow might prove too expensive to be seriously considered. She gave Barney a final hug, switched out the light, and got into bed feeling very sorry for herself, and very irritated with interfering friends.

As Mr. and Mrs. Barrett had no family of their own, Jean was in the position of an only child, and thoroughly appreciated her privileges. She was not exactly spoilt, for her uncle and aunt were absorbed with one another and with their painting, and, though they were fond of her, she did not occupy their entire attention. She just made a pleasant annex to their lives, and was treated sometimes as a child and sometimes as a grown-up, whichever happened to be the more convenient at the moment. At twelve she was a moderately tall girl, very fair, with light flaxen hair and blue eyes. Having travelled about the world so much she had rather assured manners, and was inclined to be friendly with everyone she met. There was little reserve about Jean. She chattered freely to any sympathetic listener. As she had never been to school she had few girl acquaintances, and had made no real girl friends. She had not taken readily to the French or Italian children whom she had met, her imperfect acquaintance with their languages was a decided barrier, and she had been content with the companionship of her uncle and aunt, and their artistic circle. She could always amuse herself left alone, and now she had Barney she would never lack a comrade. To change this happy state of affairs seemed to her little short of disaster.

Yet a change there was certainly going to be. Over the coffee and rolls next morning Mr. and Mrs. Barrett announced their plans. They had arranged to take the Cornish bungalow, furnished, for at least six months, or longer if they liked the place, and they would pack up and return to England almost immediately.

" We shall just be in time to leave our pictures for the Salon as we go through Paris, and for the Academy when we get to London. I've looked up the 'sending-in' dates for both," said Mr. Barrett, whose first thought was for his art. " We must have a review, Nora, and decide which is for which. I think that bit of the harbour for the Salon, and the garden scene for the Academy. That water-colour I painted of wistaria sold there last year. What a packing we shall have of all our pictures and traps."

" Terrific!" agreed Mrs. Barrett. " Still, I suppose we shall get them back somehow. The only nuisance will be the dog."

Jean dropped her knife and a dab of butter with a clatter on the floor.

" Auntie! Uncle!" she exclaimed in a voice of utter tragedy. " You couldn't leave Barney behind!"

" Poor old Jean! Your face is like a funeral!" laughed Mr. Barrett.

" I'd break my heart," choked Jean, with sudden tears in her eyes. " And he'd break his, to be given away again—when we've only just adopted him too!"

" There, there, don't worry! Nobody said we were going to leave him behind," interposed Aunt Nora. " I only said he would be a nuisance in travelling, and so he will. He'll have to go into quarantine at Dover."

" What's quarantine?"

" The same sort of thing you had when you'd played with that child who developed measles. Hydrophobia has been stamped out in England, and any dogs that are brought over from the Continent have to be put in a kind of dogs' isolation hospital for a month, to see whether they're free from the disease, before their owners are allowed to take them any farther."

" I'm sure Barney hasn't got it!"

" I don't suppose he has. But some other dog might be sickening for it, and the authorities are quite right to make the rule. Once, years ago, somebody smuggled a pet dog into England by aeroplane, and it developed hydrophobia, bit other dogs, and started the trouble again. That's why the Customs are so extremely strict. You'll have to give Barney up at Dover, and they'll put him in a Dogs' Home. I believe it's run by the Society for the Prevention of Cruelty to Animals, so he'll be well taken care of."

"And they'll charge a shilling a day for him, and we shall have to tip people, so the little beggar will cost me about two pounds for quarantine, to say nothing of going back to Dover to fetch him at the end of the month," added Mr. Barrett.

"His prize shall pay for all that," declared Jean, smiling radiantly now she knew she was not to be eternally separated from her pet.

"Well, he's a pedigree dog, and it would be a pity to part with him. You might show him in England."

"He's a beauty, Uncle. Why don't you paint his portrait and send it to the Academy?"

"Rather a good idea. Pictures of animals often sell at exhibitions. Or I might get commissions to paint other people's dogs. Would there be time, I wonder?"

"Yes, if you begin this morning," said his wife. "I think it's a capital notion of Jean's. She must sit by him and keep him quiet. It wouldn't take more than a few days, and the canvas would be dry before we start, or, at any rate, dry enough to pack in one of your stretcher cases. I always think you've rather a talent for painting animals."

"I like doing them. I'll start on this here and now! Bring your precious pet upstairs, Jean. Where is he? Chasing the cat in the garden, I expect. Go and fetch him, while I look over my paints. I hope I've a tube of brown madder. Can you lend me one, Nora, if mine is finished?"

Barney was an obedient and well trained little

dog, but posing for his portrait was a trial in the matter of keeping still. It took all Jean's authority and powers of coaxing to make him act model. The picture, dashed off in a hurry, was, however, an unqualified success. Several of Mr. Barrett's artist friends came in to look at it, and made favourable comments.

" Best you've ever done, old chap!"

" Ought to suit the Royal Academy!"

" Kind of stuff they like there."

" I bet you it sells!"

" *If* it's accepted," qualified Mr. Barrett. " Possibly it will be among the many rejected. Just my luck."

" Nonsense. The little fellow looks a perfect mascot. There's a title for the picture!"

" So it is, and a good one too. I'll call it ' The Mascot '. There's often everything in a title."

" I'm not exactly glad that Mrs. Hartley's husband was taken ill at Budapest," remarked Jean, " but it was very fortunate for us that she couldn't take Barney with her. All's for the best in this world, isn't it?"

" You unfeeling child!" laughed the guests.

Now the portrait was finished the business of packing for their departure began. As her aunt considered her more of a hindrance than help in that respect, Jean spent her time in going with Barney to say good-bye to her favourite haunts in Monaco. There was the market, with its stalls of flowers, fruit and vegetables, where the dark-eyed Italian-looking vendors had come to know the fair-haired little English girl, and always nodded pleasantly, and sometimes offered her an orange or a carnation as a gift. There were the public gardens, close to the hotel, where the gendarme, by special favour, allowed her to let her dog have a scamper without his lead, before breakfast, and there was the woman at the postcard shop near the palace, who tied a bow of blue ribbon on to Barney's collar, and expressed many hopes that they would return some day to Monaco.

Meantime her uncle and aunt, very hot and tired, endeavoured to cram their possessions into cabin trunks and suitcases.

" The Mascot!" said Mr. Barrett, as he packed his latest picture in a wooden box. " I hope it may justify its title, get into the exhibition, and bring me some commissions."

" The child has proved a mascot," said his wife. " You've had very good luck in Art since she came to us. I'm glad we didn't send the little thing away, though at the time it seemed inconvenient to have to take her about with us. She's grown up almost as much a gipsy as ourselves."

" Well, she'll have a chance to settle down for a while at Port Erbyn."

" Yes, we must certainly send her to school there, whether she likes it or not, if fees permit."

" Perhaps one mascot will pay for another," laughed Mr. Barrett, as he nailed up the box. " I painted a swastika on the reverse side of the canvas! If Barney's portrait is accepted for the Academy and sells, we may be able to afford school fees. It's on the lap of the Gods."

A few days later, after a final coffee party and leave-taking from their circle of artistic friends, the Barretts departed, with a large paraphernalia of luggage for Paris. Here they left several pictures at the " Salon des Beaux Arts ", called at one or two studios, where they had acquaintances, took a stroll through the

Musée du Louvre to refresh their memory of the " Monna Lisa " and other celebrated paintings, and next morning caught the boat-train to Calais. During the journeying Jean had been inseparable from Barney, but at Dover they were obliged to be parted. There were many formalities to be gone through about him at the Customs, and papers to be signed, and he was at length carried away by an official, looking very pathetic, while his mistress tried to blink back her tears.

" Cheer up! It's only for twenty-eight days," said Mr. Barrett. " Be thankful we haven't to leave *you* in quarantine! If you'd developed a rash on the way, they would have sent you to a fever hospital. Come along now, and we shall just have time for a cup of tea before the train starts."

" Per-per-haps he'll forget me!"

" Don't be a baby, Jean," said her aunt firmly. " You're making yourself quite ridiculous, and people are looking at you. Wipe your eyes, and come along."

London was rather a repetition of Paris. They unpacked the pictures and took them to the Royal Academy at Burlington House; they went to see a few friends, did a little necessary shopping, and set off from Paddington station for Cornwall. Port Erbyn, the place for which they were bound, was a small seaside town, with a picturesque harbour and fishing-boats, and a few quaint old streets near the quay. The bungalow was some distance away, up a steep hill, but it had a view over the sea, and a narrow lane near led to a sandy cove. Jean decided that when Barney arrived she might like it. Her uncle declared that the sketching on the whole seemed to promise well, he had already seen several good subjects. Her aunt looked anxiously round the bungalow, and said it was a great deal smaller than the Helms had given her to understand. It is always a doubtful speculation to take a house without previously inspecting it, and perhaps Mr. and Mrs. Helm's anxiety to let it had led them to describe it in rather too rosy terms. Certain obvious disadvantages had not even been mentioned. The sitting-room was artistic and pretty, there was a good studio, and three small bedrooms, scantily furnished. There was indeed a bathroom, upon which Mrs. Helm had laid much stress, but she had omitted to mention that the town pipes were not connected, and it was only supplied from a rain tank, which at the present was almost dry, and that drinking water had to be carried from a well in the lane. The stove in the kitchen was old and deficient, and most of the pans were burnt out and the crockery badly chipped. The daily maid who " did for them " was an indifferent cook, and doubted if she could " oblige " much longer, as she wished to take a place at a restaurant in Port Erbyn. The garden was rather a wilderness, with a fine crop of weeds choking the struggling flowers.

In spite of these disappointments, the Barretts were optimistic, and tried to make the best of things. They managed to secure a young girl as maid, to " live in ", and began to teach her French cookery; they renewed various breakages, and bought new pans, and set to work to put the garden into some sort of order. Having taken the bungalow for six months, they must make it as habitable as possible.

They all agreed that the neighbourhood was delightful. The soft air reminded them of Monaco, and justified its title of " the Cornish Riviera ". There was a palm tree and a myrtle outside the sitting-room window, giving rather a foreign aspect to the view, and when some of the weeds were removed, they discovered a climbing geranium that might be trained over the front door.

Mr. Barrett was at once immersed in painting; he liked the old harbour and the sailing-boats, and made sketches of some of the fishermen. Mrs. Barrett found so much to do in setting the house in order that she allowed Art to remain in abeyance for the present. Jean helped her, and quite enjoyed the experience of being in a temporary home of their own, after so much hotel life. It was quite fun to take a pail and fetch water from the well, overshadowed with ferns, that hid under a drooping ash tree in the lane. Freda, the new maid, said it was a pisky well, and that if you dropped a pin into it at sunrise, you would get a wish. Jean had not heard of Cornish piskies, but, gathering the fact that they were fairies, she asked many eager questions. Freda, a modern product of the elementary school, professed disbelief, but said her grandfather could tell many tales about them, and that the old people declared they used to see them when they were children, but never nowadays.

"Grandad says the place where your bungalow was built used to be a piskies' dancing ground," laughed Freda. "His grandmother passed in the moonlight, when she was a little girl, and there were a lot of them, all dressed in green and red. I expect it was just a field of poppies. You can fancy anything in the moonlight."

In spite of Freda's sceptical attitude towards the "realm of faery", Jean was thrilled to think of living in a pisky haunted spot. She determined to watch on the next moonlight night and to drop a pin at sunrise into the well. Unfortunately the moon was not showing just then, and she slept so soundly that she never awoke in time to welcome the dawn.

Meanwhile, more material matters engaged her attention. April was passing quickly, and very soon Barney's twenty-eight days of quarantine would be finished. Notices had come from the Royal Academy, rejecting three pictures, but accepting " The Mascot " for the exhibition.

" Well! I'm thankful that's in, at any rate," said Mr. Barrett. " I wish they'd taken the garden scene. Sorry you're out altogether, Nora!"

" I never expected any luck. When you think of the thousands of pictures that are sent in you realize it's the merest chance. Never mind! We've each got one into the Salon. I'm particularly glad about that."

" So am I. Now I have to remove our ' rejecteds ' from Burlington House, so I may as well go up to London, fetch Barney from Dover, and bring the whole cargo back here."

" Oh, Uncle Charlie! May I go with you?" begged Jean.

" Impossible, my dear. Railway fares are prohibitive. We have to study ways and means. Your school fees will just about empty the treasury till I get a fresh remittance."

" School," said Jean, pulling a face. " Why need I go to school? I don't want to, and it's an expense."

" A very necessary one," said Aunt Nora. " I'm tired of trying to teach you. I shall be thankful for somebody else to take a turn at it. You must do your best and get some knowledge into that empty little head. I'm afraid they'll find you backward, but Miss Suffolk seems prepared to have an innings, and really, it's a wonderfully nice school, from all I hear about it. She's promised not to put you in the kindergarten!

Don't look so alarmed! You'll be among girls of your own age, only you can do your individual work, and make up arrears."

" Decimals, I suppose?"

" Yes, decimals no doubt, and heaps of other things that I wasn't clever enough to teach you. I'm afraid I'd forgotten most of my own education. When I went in for Art, I let everything else slip."

" You're very nice without them, Auntie. Couldn't I let them slip too?"

" No, because there must be a background of education. Even if you forget certain facts afterwards, you must have an acquaintance with them so as to give you a general culture, and make you able to understand what other people are talking about. Otherwise you'd make absurd blunders, and they'd think you were an ignoramus. For instance, though you mayn't have learnt Latin, it would be laughable if you spoke of it as a modern language, wouldn't it?"

" I shouldn't be so silly as that. I know some French and Italian at any rate."

" You can speak them a little, but you don't know the grammar, so don't plume yourself too much on that, or you may get a snub. My advice is, be very cautious at first, and don't boast."

" Poor old Jean. You're frightening her so much she'll hardly dare to open her mouth," said Uncle Charlie. " Never mind, piccaninny, there'll be plenty of other girls who aren't too clever, I dare say. You'll have a jolly good time with the games, and I hear they go hiking in the summer. You'll like that."

" I shall be very, very thankful when my first day at school is over," replied Jean ruefully.

Mr. Barrett went to London the next week, and returned with the rejected pictures and the dog.

There was a rapturous meeting between Barney and his mistress, whom he had certainly not forgotten in the least. He approved of the freedom of the Cornish lanes, where he was seldom on his lead, and enjoyed the sandy beach of the little cove. The last week of Jean's liberty was spent in his company. Early in May she was to start work in earnest.

CHAPTER III

Jean Goes to School

Tresco House, generally called by its pupils "the little green school", on account of the creepers which covered its walls, had been run for many years by Miss Suffolk, but she had lately taken a partner, her cousin Miss Horace. The two headmistresses were exact opposites, Miss Suffolk working on rather original lines, with the idea of allowing each girl to develop her own individuality, and Miss Horace, who was a B.A. and had been a teacher at a large High School, preferring more academic methods. Between these two systems, they hoped to combine " culture " and " education ", and to turn out pupils who could enjoy a variety of interests, yet would be sufficiently up to date to cope with the requirements of modern examinations.

Tresco House was in the residential suburb of Port Erbyn, and was rather more than a mile's walk from the bungalow.

On the first day of the summer term Jean put on her new school uniform, a pale green linen dress, green knitted coat, and white hat with a green band. The shade was artistic and suited her fair hair. Her uncle and aunt looked at her with approval in their eyes. Barney had been tied to a post outside the back door, lest he should jump up and soil the freshness of her attire. She waved good-bye to him, and he barked indignantly at not being allowed to accompany her.

Jean set forth in a solemn frame of mind. Her previous wandering life had not encouraged shyness, but this was such an unexplored venture that she hardly knew how to begin, whether to seem friendly or reserved, to air her scanty accomplishments or to profess general ignorance.

" I'd better be like Brer Rabbit at first, just ' lie low and go on saying nothing '," she decided. " I'll take my cue from the others. I hope to goodness they'll be nice to me."

She arrived at Tresco House before nine. Miss Suffolk was in the garden, and conducted her first to the dressing-room, and then to a classroom, where she introduced her to several girls of about her own age, all dressed in pale-green uniforms, obviously new. There was Enid Rogers, who gave her a chilly handshake, Sheila Pritchard, who just nodded, Hope Wilkinson, who only stared, Connie Chapman, who giggled as she said " how d'you do ", Laura Bailey, who glanced at her for a moment then stooped to open a book, and Betty Tregarthen, who looked her over with twinkling brown eyes, then shook hands impulsively and warmly.

" I shall leave you to make friends," said Miss Suffolk. " One of you can show Jean her desk, and Miss Horace will give her her books by and by."

" I don't know which desk you're to have," began Enid, when the mistress had left the room. " We've chosen ours already, and there are several other girls coming who ought to have next choice. I think you and Vera had better wait and see what's left. You're both new, so it's only fair you should come last."

She turned as she spoke to a fair-haired girl who stood rather apart.

"You and Jean can sit by the window for the present," she continued. "When Mary and Grace and Nesta have come in and decided where they want to be, then we can get you settled."

"Are you Vera?" asked Jean, joining the fair-haired girl, who moved to the window as directed.

"Yes, my name's Vera Anderson. Glad I've found somebody else new. You're not a boarder, are you? I'm a weekly one. I came last night, and I'm to go home Friday to Mondays."

"Do you live at Port Erbyn?"

"No, at Lanburyan, thirty miles away. They'll fetch me in the car. Do *you* live here?"

"Not exactly ' live '. We've taken a bungalow for six months. We've only been here a month."

"Where did you come from?"

"From Monaco."

"Isn't that in the south of France? Are you French?"

"No, but we've been travelling about for years, in France and Italy mostly."

"*I've* been in France," volunteered Betty Tregarthen, who had strolled up to the window, and was listening to the conversation. "I went last summer to Bayonne and Biarritz. Look here! (in a lower voice) if there are any desks you fancy, I advise you to grab them. You've as much right to them as anybody else. They've only just been put in. It was Miss Horace's idea. Last term we all sat round a long table."

"That girl over there told us to wait," said Jean.

"Never you mind what she says. She takes too much upon herself. Miss Suffolk said we could sit where we liked. *I'd* like to sit next to you two. There are three desks in that corner. I vote we appropriate them now before anyone else gets hold of them. I'll lend you each a book to put inside. Come along!"

" You're very kind," murmured Jean, as they crossed the room and seated themselves in the places indicated by Betty.

" Oh, that's all right. I was new myself a year ago, and I haven't forgotten how Enid used to try and squash me. She always snubs new girls. You'll find you have to stand up to her. She's chosen a front desk because she likes to be in the limelight and to answer questions."

" And you've chosen a corner?"

" Because I like to keep in the background, and make a rabbit out of my pocket-handkerchief, or draw portraits inside my books, or anything else that amuses me, and I couldn't do it just under Miss Horace's eye."

Jean laughed. She was prepared to like Betty. Vera, who sat on the other side, also smiled.

" I was hoping things weren't going to be too starchy here," she remarked. " I wish you were a boarder."

" I am in winter," answered Betty. " We live on an island, and in summer I come every day by motor-boat. It isn't possible, though, after the end of October. We're often stormbound."

" Live on an island! How jolly!"

" Yes, we love it. My brothers go to school at Lestormel. Sh! sh! Here's Miss Horace. We mustn't talk any more."

Miss Horace was evidently a disciplinarian. The girls rose to their feet and said " Good morning!" in unison as she entered. The remaining members of the form had hurried in, just in time, and secured the vacant desks, after a wistful glance at Betty's corner.

Miss Horace took the roll-call, then said she hoped they liked the new arrangement of the room, which would be much more convenient than the former long table.

" I want us to have a term of very good work," she continued. " You must all try to do your best. Those of you who are new may find some of the subjects rather difficult at first, but if there is anything you can't understand, don't be afraid to ask. Come to me after school and I'll explain it. I don't expect everybody to be at the same standard, but you can all make progress if you give your best attention to the lessons. Enid, will you take these books to Vera and Jean? And these are the new geographies. Sheila, you may hand them round."

Jean opened her desk to receive the large pile of textbooks which Enid delivered, wondering privately how she would ever be able to absorb so much knowledge. They looked very formidable in contrast with the few battered lesson books she had used at Monaco. A notebook, india-rubber, pen and pencil were included, and following Vera's example, she placed these on the outside of her desk. The other girls were examining the new geographies with interest, but Miss Horace told them to put them away now, and plunged into a lecture on history. It was instructive but rather dry. Jean's information was so hazy that she had little idea whether Charles II was a Plantagenet or a member of the House of Hanover. She had neglected to learn the dates of the kings of England, which ought to have accompanied her acquaintance with the multiplication table and weights and measures. Still, she gleaned some facts about the Commonwealth, the battle of Worcester, and the subsequent escape of the fugitive monarch.

Seeing that the other girls were taking notes she

seized her pencil and jotted down something whenever Miss Horace made the necessary pauses for that purpose. It seemed well to look business-like, and as if she were accustomed to school routine. Betty scribbled away busily, and Vera also was making entries.

It was a warm morning, and the French window stood wide open. From the garden came the scent of lilac and the song of a blackbird. Everything was very calm and quiet and scholastic. Miss Horace was discoursing upon English politics during the Commonwealth, and the form was listening intently, with open notebooks ready for the next pause. Then suddenly, like the shock of an earthquake, came a violent interruption. There was a scramble, a delighted yelp, and through the open window bounded Barney, rushing under desks to Jean's corner, where he jumped up with dirty paws upon her clean green linen dress. Mary's little lamb could not have caused more consternation. Miss Horace stopped in the middle of a sentence. The girls turned to gaze and giggle. Barney barked triumphantly, and his luckless mistress blushed crimson with confusion.

" Is that your dog, Jean?" asked Miss Horace.

" Yes. Oh, I'm so sorry! Down, Barney, down!" gasped Jean. " I tied him up before I left home, and he must have bitten through his lead and tracked me to school."

The frayed leather strap, dangling from the little dog's collar, was a testimony to the truth of her statement. Barney seemed immensely proud of his achievement.

" What am I to do with him?" asked Jean anxiously. " I'm so very sorry."

" You must shut him up inside the toolshed in the garden," replied Miss Horace. " Betty will show you where it is. Go with her, Betty, and put the padlock on the door of the shed. And be as quick as you possibly can."

Jean seized her tempestuous pet and carried him away, amid smiles from the form and a look of patient annoyance from Miss Horace. With Betty's help she hustled him into the toolshed, called him a naughty dog, and told him to lie down.

" Rather clever of the poor little chap to find you out here, wasn't it?" remarked Betty, producing a piece of milk chocolate from her pocket and offering it to Barney. " He'll be safe enough here. I'll padlock the door. The gardener won't be likely to come in till twelve o'clock. He's mowing the grass this morning. Now we must scoot, or we shall get into disgrace."

" I'm afraid I'm in disgrace now. It's a bad beginning."

" Well, you couldn't help it. You tied him up."

" I shall have to buy a chain that he can't bite through."

" And so the teacher turned him out;
It was against the rule,"

chanted Betty. " You must train him to ' wait patiently about ' till you come out of school. We should have a zoo here if our pets all followed us. Now then, look crushed and sorry, and I expect Miss Horace will forgive you."

" Shall I apologize at once?"

" No, no, go to your desk, and don't interrupt the lesson. You can beg pardon afterwards, and explain how it happened. Hurry up, or *I* shall get the blame!"

At the end of a morning's bewildering work Jean felt there were so many things she could not understand that Miss Horace would need to spend hours in explanation if she began to ask questions. She ran after the teacher, however, and apologized for Barney's misdoings.

" It shan't happen again. I'll lock him up at home," she said contritely. " What am I to do with him now?"

" You may take him a little run round the garden, and we'll give him some dinner, then he must go back to the toolshed again till four o'clock. Now, about your lessons, Jean. I'm afraid you're rather backward. You'll need some special coaching in mathematics. Your French is above the average, but you'll have to work hard at your English subjects. You must give an hour and a half every evening to your preparation, and do it in a room alone, where people aren't talking, and don't have the dog with you, to take away your attention."

" I won't. Though he sits quite quietly when I tell him to lie down."

" I wouldn't trust him," laughed Miss Horace. " You'll study far better without a dog in the room."

It had been arranged for Jean to take midday dinner at school. To walk home to the bungalow and back would be too great a hurry, and her uncle and aunt were so occupied with their sketching and so unpunctual, that they did not wish to fix a definite time for lunch, and preferred to have it at their own convenience. Often they took sandwiches with them and did not return till tea. It was rather a relief to them to know that Jean was well occupied at Tresco House for the whole day, and that they need not interrupt their painting on her behalf. Also, it would give her an opportunity of making friends with her schoolfellows. Several others of the girls were daily boarders, and during recreation, before afternoon work, they spent their leisure in the garden.

Jean decided quickly that she did not care much for Enid and Sheila, who kept themselves decidedly aloof, that Laura was patronizing, that Connie was amusing, and that Betty, with her merry brown eyes, and jolly, hearty manners, was the nicest of them all. She was the only one who had really extended a welcome. Vera, as a newcomer, was still rather shy, but Jean thought she was going to like Vera. There was something particularly attractive about her. Moreover, she was fond of dogs, and said she had a fox terrier at home. After Barney had demolished a plateful of dinner, the three girls took him a walk round the garden. He was very subdued and ashamed of himself and kept well to heel.

" Miss Horace says I mustn't have him with me when I'm learning my lessons," explained Jean. " She says I'm to do an hour and a half's preparation every evening in a room quite by myself!"

" An hour and a half! That's rather stiff!" exclaimed Betty.

" How much do you do?"

" Only an hour. We're none of us supposed to do more."

" Then it's because I'm so backward."

" Poor you!"

" Is Miss Horace rather a tartar?" asked Vera.

" Well, no, not exactly. She's fearfully keen on making us work though. We didn't like her at all when first she came, but she's much jollier than she seems when you get to know her."

" What about Miss Suffolk?"

" She's a dear. She gives the most delightful lessons. We all enjoy them. Only you see she doesn't care about preparing us for exams and that sort of thing.

That doesn't trouble *me*—I hate exams. But some of the girls' parents thought they ought to go in for the School Certificate later on, so that was why Miss Suffolk took a partner. Miss Horace is a good coach. Enid and Sheila and Laura are working hard with her. They like her way of teaching. Miss Suffolk suits me better. I don't want to go to college and take my B.A. I'm going to help Dad with flower farming when I'm old enough. It'll be far more fun. What are you going to do, Jean, when you're grown up?"

Jean shook her head. " I haven't the least idea," she confessed. " My uncle and aunt are artists."

" Can you paint?"

" Not very well. I try a little, but I don't think I'm clever at it."

" I should like to go on the stage, or act for the films," announced Vera. " I love acting."

" Do you? Then you'll just suit Miss Suffolk. You'll get a chance this afternoon, at the history lesson."

" The history lesson?" echoed Vera, in amazement.

" Yes, just you wait and see! No, I haven't time to explain now. We must put this dog back in the toolshed. It's nearly half-past two. Sheila's calling to us. All right, Sheila—we're coming!"

After again locking up Barney, the three girls ran into the house and took their places at their desks in the schoolroom. Miss Suffolk entered almost immediately and the class began.

The two partners worked in co-operation—Miss Horace taking the practical side and the hard facts of a subject, and Miss Suffolk supplying the imaginative side. That morning the girls had studied a portion of the period of the Commonwealth, learning dates of battles and names of leaders; what might be described as the skeleton of the subject. This afternoon they were to try to make the dry bones live.

Miss Suffolk first read them a spirited account of the escape of Charles II after the defeat of his army at Worcester, and some of his romantic adventures before he embarked to France.

" Now," she concluded, " we'll go into the garden and act this. I shall give you five minutes to talk it over and choose your parts. The old apple tree will do for the oak. We'll start there. The schoolroom can be Packington Hall, afterwards."

The class rose at once and filed in orderly fashion into the garden, where they held a kind of committee meeting, rapidly suggesting details.

" Betty had better be Charles, because she climbs so well," said Enid. " I'll be Colonel John Lane, and Sheila can be Jane. Connie, Laura, and Maisie can be Roundhead soldiers, and the rest of you can be villagers at first, and Puritans afterwards, when we want the troops at Packington. Run behind that bush, Betty! Iva, you may be the messenger to bring the news. Are you all ready? Here's Miss Suffolk."

Not quite understanding what was required from them, Jean and Vera nevertheless took their places with others under the apple tree. Iva, showing much agitation, ran up to them and announced the ill news that the battle was lost, and the King, hotly pursued by Cromwell's troopers, was hurrying to them for protection. They all earnestly protested their loyalty, but feared they could not hide him in their cottages, which would be sure to be searched by the soldiers. Betty, apparently panting with fatigue, rushed into their midst, and was received with enthusiasm.

" Up the tree, your Majesty!" shouted Phyllis, " the thick leaves will hide you. Quick, quick! I can hear the sound of horses' hoofs. Those rascals will be here in a minute."

Betty scrambled into the apple tree with dexterity, and had just reached a convenient fork when the troopers arrived, hot on the scent, and began to question the villagers, who denied having seen any fugitive, but offered to allow their houses to be searched. The soldiers, having departed on this fruitless errand, the King climbed down again, and was hurried away by Colonel John Lane, who came to his rescue from behind a hedge. The class then adjourned to the school-room, which was supposed to represent Packington Hall. Jane Lane, in a speech full of loyalty and enthusiasm, offered to aid the King to escape if he would condescend to disguise himself as her servant, and ride with her to Bristol. He was accepting her brave offer when again there was a warning of danger. Troopers were coming to search the old mansion. He must hide in the secret hiding-place. The book cupboard made a handy substitute for this, and Betty was crammed inside and the door shut upon her, while the Parliamentary soldiers strode about among the desks, shouting what they would do with the renegade when they caught him.

"His head shall fall like his father's!" declared Connie, with bloodthirsty zeal.

"So perish all the enemies of the Commonwealth!" said Laura, in unctuous Puritan tones.

When the troopers had moved on, Betty, very hot and cramped, was allowed to emerge from the cupboard, was informed that a horse was at the door, and that Mistress Jane would ride pillion behind him. His Majesty then thanked his devoted subjects, who knelt and kissed his royal hand, and with a parting injunction from Colonel John Lane to remember his character as a man-servant, and not to betray himself under any circumstances, he was escorted by Mistress Jane into the garden, and the scene was over.

Jean had enjoyed it very much, though she took little part. Vera had at once seemed to enter into the spirit of it, and had joined in the conversations with great animation.

" Can't we go on any further with his escape?" she asked.

" No, we're to do handicrafts now," answered Sheila. " We're to stencil bags this afternoon. Have you done any stencilling before?"

" *I* have," said Jean. " I'm rather fond of it. My uncle showed me how to cut them."

" I say! I like your history lessons if this is a specimen," declared Vera. " It was ever such fun putting Betty into the cupboard. Where is Packington Hall?"

" That's just the question I hoped you would ask," said Miss Suffolk. " It's in Warwickshire, not far from Coventry. Don't *you* want to ask anything, Jean?"

" I suppose they got safely to Bristol? What became of Mistress Jane?"

" She married Sir Clement Fisher, the owner of Packington Hall, and at the Restoration she received a pension as a reward for her services to the King when he was a fugitive."

" She deserved it."

" Shall you remember about King Charles's escape now?"

" Yes, indeed I shall. But—I'm afraid I've forgotten the date of the battle of Worcester!"

" Oh, Jean! 1651. I'm sure Miss Horace made you write that in your notes this morning?"

" I believe she did. I've no head for dates."

"You must try and improve your memory. My dramatic history lessons won't be of much use unless they help you to visualize English history, and you can't do that without some knowledge of your periods. We don't act these little scenes just for play. Here comes Miss Bond for handicrafts. You have two new pupils, Miss Bond—Jean Barrett and Vera Anderson. I believe they're both artistic, so you can set them to work on bags."

"I like Miss Suffolk," whispered Vera, as the headmistress left the classroom. "She's so human, somehow, not a bit starchy."

"I think she's an absolute dear," agreed Jean.

CHAPTER IV

The Bathing Cove

At the end of the afternoon Enid, who was head girl and considered herself responsible for the form, finding Jean fumbling helplessly in her desk, sorted out the books she would need for her evening preparation, and packed them in a canvas bag.

" Mind you bring back the bag to-morrow morning," she commanded. " It's a special favourite of mine. I did the raffia pattern myself. You must ask your aunt to find you a bag of your own for your books. Are you going to fetch your dog now? I hope he won't follow you to school again to-morrow!"

" I'll take good care he shan't."

" Miss Horace was very nice about him, but, of course, she doesn't like the lesson interrupted. We none of us do."

" I couldn't help it," said Jean meekly.

She looked round to say good-bye to Betty, but Betty had already gone to the harbour to catch the motor-boat to her island, and Vera also had disappeared. So Jean released Barney and turned her footsteps homewards. She arrived at the bungalow in time for tea, full of her day's experiences.

" Well? How did you get on at school?" asked her

uncle, handing her the strawberry jam. " Barney played you a nasty trick! We left him tied up when we went out sketching. We took our lunch with us and weren't back till nearly four, and then found him gone. We thought Freda must have taken him for a walk."

" I'm afraid Miss Suffolk wouldn't bargain for a dog as an extra pupil," laughed Aunt Nora.

" She didn't scold, nor Miss Horace either. They knew it wasn't my fault. Oh, I got on all right. Miss Suffolk's history lesson was jolly. Miss Horace makes everybody work very hard. She says I must do an hour and a half's preparation every evening."

" Miss Suffolk told me only an hour was required," said Mrs. Barrett.

" That's all the rest of the girls do, but it's because I'm so backward."

" They mustn't work you too hard, especially just at first," objected Uncle Charlie.

" I expect I've got my nose to the grindstone now," sighed Jean. " I'll show you what a lot of books I've brought home. You'll be really sorry for me when you see them."

Jean made a conscientious attack on her preparation that evening, but if Aunt Nora had not helped her, she would have found it very difficult. She was not accustomed to adjust her work, and would have given too much time to one subject and too little to another. However, between them, they went over the various portions marked, till Uncle Charlie called out that it was eight o'clock, and if they were not ready for supper he was, anyhow.

Jean set off for school next morning with Enid's bag, empty, on one arm, and a leather bag of her own, containing her books, on the other. She got on better than she had expected in her classes, and received half an hour's private tuition from Miss Horace to coach her in the mysteries of decimals. Betty and Vera gave her surreptitious help now and then, and when it came to the French lesson she was guilty of prompting them with an occasional word.

" I say!" remarked Vera afterwards, " you know French jolly well."

" I've been so much in France," said Jean. " I had to talk a certain amount there, so I can get along in speaking it, but I'm stumped when it comes to the grammar or the dictation."

" Weren't you at school in France then?"

" No. I live with my uncle and aunt. They're both artists, and they travel about a great deal. We've been in Italy too."

" Haven't you a father and mother, or brothers and sisters?"

" No."

" No more have I. I live with my grandfather and grandmother, thirty miles from here. I used to go every day to a small school near home. Then Grannie heard of Tresco House, and insisted on sending me. I bargained I should come back for the week-ends, though. I said it would be the only thing to save my life!"

" The little green school isn't half bad," put in Betty, who was listening. " I'm a boarder in the winter, and I just get a week-end at home now and then, when the sea's smooth. It's the same with the boys."

" You have brothers?" asked Vera.

" Two. I wouldn't be without them for worlds. I should hate to be a ' one and only '."

" Oh, I like it," said Vera. " It's lovely to think

there's nobody else. I get all the petting and spoiling. I shouldn't want to divide it up. I'd be fearfully jealous if Grandad and Grannie had anyone else to fuss over except me! That's that, and I don't mind saying so!"

"Well! It's one way of looking at it, at any rate. You're certainly frank!" said Betty. "What about you, Jean?"

"When you haven't got anything it's as well to take things just as they are," remarked Jean philosophically.

School had opened on a Tuesday, and Wednesday afternoon was always given up to sports, so on this second day the time from three o'clock onwards would be somewhat in the nature of a holiday. Last term the girls had played hockey, but this term they would devote themselves to cricket and tennis. As it happened, however, to be extremely warm weather, quite an unusual heat wave, Miss Horace decided to take her elder pupils that afternoon to a cove near, for a swimming practice.

"Brought your bathing costume, Jean?" inquired Enid, when dinner was over.

"No, I didn't know we were going to bathe."

"I thought I told you yesterday."

"You certainly didn't."

"Well, I meant to anyway. What's to be done about it?"

"Have I time to sprint home and fetch mine?"

"No, I'm sure you haven't. You see, we start work at a quarter past two on Wednesdays, so as to get a class in before three o'clock."

"So it isn't to be all holiday," complained Jean.

"It's sports after three, if that's what you mean. We don't call it a holiday. We get that on Saturday.

Now I'm worried about your bathing costume. I wonder if Sheila has her old one here? Sheila! Sheila! I want you—hurry up!"

Sheila strolled leisurely to the group.

" What's the excitement?" she inquired.

" Jean hasn't her bathing costume here."

" Well, I'm afraid she won't be allowed to bathe without it!"

" Oh, don't be silly. What I want to know is, have you kept the old one you had last year? And will you lend it to her?"

" I believe it's somewhere or other."

" Then go and find it. It's probably in the cupboard on the stairs. Be quick! It's nearly a quarter past two now."

" All right! All right! I'm going. What a fusser you are, Enid."

" I'm sorry to be a nuisance," put in Jean. " Could *I* find it?"

" No, I'm sure you couldn't, for I don't quite know where it is myself. But I'll have a hunt anyhow. I'll probably turn it up."

" Thanks so much."

" Better not thank me till I've found it," laughed Sheila. " I'm not a tidy person, and I never know where my things are."

" She *does* know—she's just putting it on," commented Enid, as Sheila walked away, without any undue hurry. " She does it to tease me. She'll find it all right, you'll see. We needn't worry."

Enid's remarks were justified, for in a few minutes, just before the bell rang for afternoon school, Sheila sauntered back with a blue bathing costume and a scarlet rubber cap.

" The piskies just popped them into my hand,"

she said. " They were at the top of a pile in the cupboard."

" It's ever so good of you to lend them," rejoiced Jean.

" Oh, you're welcome, I'm sure. They're no use to me now. I've grown out of that costume. Miss Suffolk will lend you a towel."

For three quarters of an hour the girls concentrated their attention on a lesson in algebra, then when the clock struck three they thankfully put their books inside their desks and fetched their bathing equipment. Only the seniors were going this afternoon. They started off in charge of Miss Horace. They walked a short way along the headland, then down a steep path on the cliffside to a small cove. It was a retired, sheltered place, and though in August it would be filled with visitors, at this early season of the year they had it almost to themselves. There were only a few nurses and children on the sands, and a couple of sun-bathers, trying to bake themselves brown. They undressed behind the rocks, and were soon taking their first plunges into the water.

Jean had often bathed in the Mediterranean, and was quite a good swimmer. Miss Horace would not accept her testimony on that score without personal observation, however, and kept her near to her until she was satisfied that she would not be likely to get into difficulties. Betty seemed as agile as a fish or a seal in the sea. She came swimming up to Jean, and began to perform some stunts.

" Oh, I wish I could do that!" cried the latter admiringly.

" Betty lives on an island, and gets plenty of practice," said Enid. " She bathes every day when she's at home. Don't you, Betty?"

" Rather! Harry and Michael and I spend half our time in the water during the hols."

" Even in winter?"

" Yes, even in winter sometimes, if there's not an east wind."

" Isn't the water very cold?"

" Not too cold for us."

" Do you find this chilly, Jean?" asked Miss Horace.

" A little."

" I was afraid you might, after being used to the Mediterranean. Go ashore, and take a run on the beach, and then try a dive."

As a matter of fact, Jean found the Cornish water exceedingly cold. She came out shivering and rather blue, and was glad to race about in the sunshine. She was joined presently by Vera, who announced that it was her first bathe that year.

" We don't live near the sea at home," she said, " so I haven't had as much chance as these girls. I can swim a little though."

" Can you dive?"

" Well, I have done once."

" It's quite easy."

" Is it?"

" Yes, you just put up your arms, this way."

On the rocks at the end of the beach, some planks had been arranged to make a diving board, and several of the girls were running along these and taking headers into a pool below.

" Come along, you two!" called Connie. " We're going to have ' follow the leader '. Betty! Betty! Come here! You shall be leader. We'll all try and do what you do."

Betty came ashore in response to this summons, and putting herself at the head of a small line of girls, scampered off towards the diving board. Connie was next to her, then Jean, and Vera, followed by Peggie White and Grace Appleton.

Now Vera, carried away by the enthusiasm of the others, was not at all sure of herself. She had only tried to dive once before. She did not like to confess her timidity, or to fall out of the line, but she ran along the plank feeling a thorough coward. Betty took a magnificent plunge from the end, Connie followed with one almost equally good, and Jean also made a successful third. It was now Vera's turn, and she stood shivering on the brink! Peggy was behind her, and Peggie was not at all disposed to be kept waiting.

" Go on, stupid—what are you sticking there for?" cried Peggy, giving her a vigorous push.

Poor Vera was not prepared for the onslaught. Instead of diving she lost her balance and tumbled with a tremendous splash into the pool below. She rose to the surface spluttering and thinking herself half drowned. Jean made a dash for her and held her up till she could get her breath, and Betty and Connie, who were frolicking farther out in the water, swam back to see what was the matter. Peggie, seated on the end of the diving board, shouted mocking remarks as they hauled Vera to land.

" You looked just like a porpoise! Is that a new way of diving?"

" You're a horrid girl—you pushed me in," returned Vera indignantly.

" Oh, that's how they teach puppies to swim. You always throw a pup into the sea and let it find its way back!"

" What's all this about?" asked Miss Horace, joining the party on the beach.

" Peggie pushed Vera off the diving board, and she tumbled in."

" We've been doing life saving!"

" It was good practice."

" Do you know how to dive, Vera?" asked Miss Horace.

" Not very well," confessed Vera, who was still coughing and ejecting sea water, and feeling sorry for herself.

" I'll give you a lesson presently. As for you, Peggie, you may go and get dressed and walk back to school. I can't have you pushing people into the water. Go at once!"

Rather sulkily Peggie obeyed. Miss Horace was not to be trifled with. The rules, moreover, for bathing practice were strict, and she knew she had transgressed.

" I don't like Peggie White," said Vera afterwards to Jean. " There's something mocking about her. *You're* a sport. You came double quick and held me up. I'd rather not try diving again this afternoon. I hope Miss Horace won't offer to teach me."

Miss Horace was discreet enough to notice that her pupil had had sufficient for that day, and very soon gave the signal for all the girls to come out of the water. She had left a whistle on the rocks, and she now blew it as a summons.

" We haven't been in long," objected Enid.

" Long enough for a first bathe. Remember it's only May and the water is rather cold. Give yourselves a good brisk rub with your towels, and dress as fast as you can. Don't loiter. You shall have some hot tea when we get back to school."

As she thought Jean looked blue and chilly, and the bungalow was a mile away, Miss Horace invited her to have tea with the boarders on their return to the school. She was very careful about the health of her pupils, and knowing Jean had spent the winter on the Riviera, she feared Cornish waters had proved too cold for her.

The meal was ready, and Jean certainly found the hot drink most acceptable. It was a new experience to have tea with the teachers and the boarders. She sat next to Vera, who looked after her and handed her the cake. Miss Suffolk was extremely jolly and asked riddles. Even Miss Horace, whom Jean had hitherto regarded as very scholastic, waxed quite jovial and made a pun.

" I thought we shouldn't be allowed to speak," whispered Jean to Vera.

" Oh, we talk. We're just like a big family. Only, of course, we mustn't do anything outrageous. Peggie threw a pellet of bread across the table at Enid yesterday, and Miss Suffolk sent her straight out of the room."

Peggie, who sat near, overheard, and pulled a face at Vera.

" Who's telling tales about me?" she snapped.

Enid, from the opposite side of the table, quickly changed the subject of conversation.

" Are you fond of tennis, Jean?" she asked.

" I love it. We played a good deal last winter at Monaco. On a cinder court, of course."

" Ours is a cinder court, too. It's a new one. Will it be ready by next week, Miss Horace?"

" I hope so. Mr. Jago has been a very long time making it. It was promised for Easter."

" Port Erbyn people don't always keep their promises in that respect," laughed Miss Suffolk. " How long was it before the greenhouse door was mended?"

" A whole month, and we had to board up the broken window."

" The new roller has come, so the court can be rolled," said Miss Horace.

" Oh! when did it arrive?" cried the boarders.

" This afternoon. I sent a message to Mr. Jago at once."

" I'm glad you can play tennis, Jean," said Enid. " We want to get up some good sets."

" Yes, indeed, it will be our first term for tennis on a court of our own," continued Miss Horace. " You'll all have to practise hard and get into training."

" Can we have a tournament later on, with some other school?" inquired Sheila.

" I must see how you can play before we begin to think about tournaments. We shouldn't like to be badly beaten for a start."

" I played in a girls' tournament at Monaco," said Jean. " I had a Danish girl for a partner, and she was splendid."

" Oh, did you win?"

" No, but we made quite good scores. Two French girls from the Lycée won the prizes. They were the champion players of their school. I never saw such quick serving."

" Well, I hope you'll be a help to us here," said Miss Horace. " You must come sometimes on Saturday afternoons and practise."

Enid, who had hitherto almost ignored Jean, was now looking at her with newly awakened interest. Enid was Miss Horace's greatest ally in reorganizing the school on modern methods. She wanted to have everything up to date, to compete with other schools in games, and to go in for public examinations. While some of the girls preferred Miss Suffolk's rather singular modes of education, she was all in favour of the new régime. Vera also was smiling at her neighbour.

"So glad you like tennis," she whispered. "I was beginning to think this was a rotten school, but I'm cheered up now. Between tennis and the bathing I shall survive. I wish you were a boarder. We can get some sets before afternoon school, though, I expect most days. Have you a nice racquet?"

"A1. It was a birthday present," returned Jean.

CHAPTER V

Jean Remembers

May was a happy and exciting month at the bungalow. Jean was interested in her school work, and Mr. and Mrs. Barrett were delighted with the sketching at Port Erbyn. A very good piece of news arrived one morning. The portrait of Barney had been sold at the Academy. Mr. Barrett was immensely encouraged.

" Good dog!" he exclaimed. " Beg nicely and you shall have a piece of bacon. You deserve it. You've really proved a mascot."

" I believe the title of the picture was half the battle," said Aunt Nora, " though it's one of the best you've ever done."

" Well, I'm glad it will have a red star on it in the exhibition."

" You'll have to try painting Barney again," said Jean. " He looks very jolly when he begs. You might call it ' The Beggar '."

" Not such a bad title either," admitted her uncle. " I must think about it some day."

Then there was another excitement. Mr. Barrett's mother had died a year ago, and a few of the things from her house had been left to him. As he had been abroad ever since it had not been possible for him to have them, but now that he was temporarily settled at Port Erbyn, the executor wrote to say that he was dispatching a large packing case to the bungalow, containing some silver, books and other possessions.

The case arrived while Jean was at school and was carried into the studio. When she returned at half-past four her uncle and aunt were busy unpacking, and were opening parcels and spreading a variety of articles over the table. They were so engrossed with their occupation, that they did not hear Jean enter the room. Mrs. Barrett was rejoicing over antique Georgian teaspoons, and her husband was looking through a pile of books and papers. Both had their backs to Jean.

" Hello! What have I got here?" said Mr. Barrett, holding out a cabinet photograph. " Surely this is my brother Jim! Jim and his family. Taken at Vancouver before they went to Alaska."

Jean, standing by the door and looking across, could see the photograph quite well. It showed a dark-haired man, in clerical collar, a dark-haired lady, and four dark-haired children, taken together in a group.

Mrs. Barrett gazed at it contemplatively.

" Yes, not much resemblance to our fair little Jean there," she remarked. " She certainly wasn't one of *them*!"

Jean walked quietly up behind her uncle.

" *That's* not my daddy!" she exclaimed. " It can't be. Daddy and Mummie were both very fair."

Mr. and Mrs. Barrett started, and turned with the utmost consternation in their faces. Aunt Nora snatched the photo and pushed it underneath some papers.

" I didn't know you had come in, Jean," she said. " We're busy unpacking. Go and tell Freda to make the tea. Run and pick a bunch of flowers from the garden and put them on the table. I hear Barney barking outside. He wants a game with you. Go and play with him till tea's ready."

Thus summarily banished, Jean walked into the garden in much bewilderment. Strange remembrances of her early childhood were stirring, remembrances half forgotten but still remaining in her subconscious mind. Her uncle and aunt never talked of that time in her life before she came to live with them. She knew instinctively that it was a subject to which they did not wish her to refer. Mr. Barrett's only brother had been a missionary among the Indians in North America and had died there. It was natural that his child should be sent home to her uncle and aunt. She could recall her arrival in England, and how they had met her at the steamer and taken her away with them. She had been very young then, and so frightened of strangers. She had cried piteously in the train, and they had comforted her with chocolates.

" But—but—" mused Jean, struggling to understand tangled memories. " Daddy and Mummie were fair, and there were no other children—only me! That dark man and dark lady in the photo weren't Daddy and Mummie."

Barney's tempestuous welcome interrupted her perplexed thoughts, and the tea bell soon followed to call her indoors. No further reference was made to the episode, though when Aunt Nora took her into the studio later on to show her the antique silver and a few trinkets, she noticed that all the papers had been put away. A pile of books still remained, which her uncle began hastily to arrange on a shelf.

" Some of my old school prizes, Jean," he said. " You wouldn't guess I'd ever won prizes, would you? I'm afraid I've forgotten most of what I learnt.

I was very proud of them at the time. Look! They have the school crest on the covers."

" I like the bindings. They smell nice," said Jean.

" Yes, the prizes were always well bound. I used to like the outsides more than the insides of them. They were all classics, and I never was a book-worm. I preferred *Treasure Island* to *Bacon's Essays* or the plays of Euripides. Perhaps you'll be bringing back prizes some day from Tresco House."

" I don't believe they give any. And I'm sure I shouldn't win any if they did."

" Well, never mind. Prizes aren't everything. The boys and girls who get them at school don't always do the best in the world afterwards. Where are you off to now? Your preparation? I thought you were coming with us to the cove? We're going to paint the sunset. Can't you bring your books and sit on the rocks?"

Jean shook her head sorrowfully.

" I'd love to, but I know I shouldn't do a scrap of work. Miss Horace says I can't ' focus my attention '. She made me promise to do my prep in a room quite by myself, without even Barney being there."

" Well, well! I suppose she knows how to make you learn your lessons. But it's hard on a fine evening like this. Nora! This poor kid has to shut herself up and swot over decimals or something of the kind."

" Oh, no, Uncle. I can do decimals quite easily now," laughed Jean. " Miss Horace explained them. It's English literature and botany to-night, and a French exercise."

" Good luck to you then. We're just off. You can walk down the lane and join us if you've finished before we're back. Come along, Nora, are you ready?"

Jean spent her allotted time over her preparation,

and hesitated whether she should follow her uncle and aunt to the cove. She had almost decided to do so when her eyes fell on the prizes which she had helped to arrange on the shelf. It would amuse her to look at them, even if their contents were more classical than entertaining. She turned over the pages, taking up one book after another. At the end of the row was another morocco-bound volume, rather different from the rest. It proved to be, not a prize, but a family Bible, and from its inscription, had evidently belonged to her uncle's mother. Her name, Margaret Barrett, was written on the fly leaf, with a list of her children, the dates of their births and marriages, and the names of their children. There was Rosamond, who married Percy Howell, and had a son, with " died in infancy " written underneath. There was Charles, who married Nora Muriel Cotman, and there was James, who married Hilda Norman, and had four children, Arthur, Leonard, Bertha, and Daisy. This last family was bracketed together with red ink, and a note added " all perished by epidemic in Canada ". Jean turned over the fly leaf, but there were no more entries. Her own name was not among the list of the Barretts.

She thrust the Bible back to its place on the shelf, and stood pondering.

" It's no use. I've been silent too long. I *do* remember things. I shall have to ask Aunt Nora and *make* her tell me! I've a right to know. I'm not a little child now. I'm a girl of twelve. There's some secret that they've kept from me. I always guessed there was. I've half found it out now, but not quite. Uncle Charlie would only laugh and dodge my questions. I'll get Auntie when she's alone, and try and have a serious talk and tell her all I remember. Then perhaps I can persuade her to explain what's so very puzzling about it all."

Jean found no opportunity either that evening or for several days to have a private talk with her aunt. Uncle Charlie always seemed to be there, or friends, whom they had made at Port Erbyn, came in for a chat and stayed late. The Bible, from which she had gleaned her information, disappeared off the shelf next morning. Evidently it had been put away. Jean went about looking dreamy and preoccupied. She found it difficult to concentrate her thoughts upon her lessons. In the midst of her classes at school her mind would drift far back among a confused mist of old memories, and she would start when a question was asked her. Miss Horace reprimanded her several times for her lack of attention, and even Miss Suffolk inquired if she was not feeling well, and urged her to put more heart into her work. At home she was unusually quiet, and would sit cuddling Barney instead of running round the garden and throwing him his ball.

Aunt Nora looked at her uneasily sometimes, but made no remark. Uncle Charlie seemed to make more jokes than ever, as if he were trying to keep her amused.

It was not until Sunday evening that Jean found her chance. Her uncle had gone to Port Erbyn to call on an artist acquaintance, and for once she had her aunt to herself. They went a little walk together and sat down on a log underneath an oak tree in a field. Words were burning on Jean's lips, but for a while she had not the courage to utter them. Then suddenly she made the plunge.

"Auntie! There's something I want to ask you about. Something I can't understand. How is it that my name's not in the family Bible? There's no

' Jean ' written in it. I thought my daddy was Uncle Charlie's only brother? But that photo wasn't in the least like my daddy. And I hadn't any brothers or sisters. Surely I should have remembered them if I had? I've forgotten so much, but not everything. Bits of things are in my mind, and then blanks, and then more bits, only I can't put them together. It's like fitting in the pieces of a jig-saw puzzle to make a picture."

Mrs. Barrett put her arm very tenderly round Jean's shoulder.

" Will you tell me, dear, just exactly what you *do* remember?" she asked.

So Jean began.

" I can remember being very little, and playing in a beautiful garden where there were heaps of lovely roses. There was a tank with big white flowers in it, water-lilies I suppose, and I liked to walk round the edge of it, but someone always held my hand. There was a lady, and a gentleman, they were both very fair. I'm sure I called them Daddy and Mummie. The gentleman used to carry me on his shoulder. The lady had golden hair, and she came to kiss me at night, when I was in bed. There was a dog too. It was so big that I had rides on its back. There were no other children there. I was the only one. It just seems like a dream.

" Then there's a big blank, and the next thing I remember is being in a long queer kind of boat, and Indians rowing it. We were on a great wide river, with a forest on each side of it. We landed at one place, but there was a bear, and Mummie was so frightened she caught me up in her arms and got back into the boat, and I heard Daddy shooting, and the Indians shouted. I remember our boat going between high walls of rock, and the water being very rough, and we rushed along, with the Indians paddling hard, and I sat on Mummie's knee, and she held me so tight. Then there's another blank, and it was very cold, with snow falling. The Indians and the boat had gone, and Mummie and I were alone in a small hut. She kept putting wood into a stove. We heard something scratching outside the door, and Mummie was terribly afraid, and kept wishing Daddy would come back.

" Then there's a big black blank. Everything seems confused afterwards. The next thing that comes clearly to me is that I was living among the Indians in their tents. I was afraid of the men, they looked so wild, but the women gave me food. Some of the children didn't like me, and threw snow at me, but one old woman was kind, and she wouldn't let them hurt me. She said I was lucky. We used to go sliding over the snow on long pieces of wood. There were dogs, too, and sledges, and sometimes we heard wolves. It makes me shudder to think of that howling, even now.

" Then there's another big blank. Somebody came and took me away, a long way down the river, and then in a ship. A great many people—white people—talked to me, and someone gave me a doll. But I was so frightened of them all. They kept asking me questions, and I couldn't answer them. I could scarcely understand what they were saying to me. I remember being in a big house with a great many children, and eating porridge out of a wooden bowl. I didn't like it, but somebody in a white cap smacked me if I didn't finish it all.

" Then I can remember going in a train, and being in a big steamer on the sea. My memory about that is a little clearer. I used to play games on deck, throwing rings into a bucket, and tossing a ball about. It was very rough once, and they put racks on the table to keep the plates and dishes from tumbling about. The vessel rolled so much that I fell down the stairs and hurt my arm, and the doctor bandaged it up and put it in a sling. I couldn't play games properly afterwards, because I could only use one arm.

" Then the steamer landed, and you and Uncle Charlie came on board, and said you were my uncle and aunt, and I must go away with you. But I didn't know you, and I cried, and wanted to stay with some other children and with their mother. You took me in the train, and I kept on crying, and Uncle Charlie gave me chocolates, and you showed me some pictures in a book. Then there's another big blank. After that I remember everything quite well. I was living with you and Uncle Charlie in France. The rest is clear enough, but that first part seems like dreams. That's all."

" Now I'll take up my side of the story, and tell you what I know," said Mrs. Barrett gently, when Jean had finished. So she began:

" My husband had only one brother, James, who was a clergyman, and went as a missionary to the West Indies. He was married out there, to an American missionary, and they had four children, two boys and two girls. I never saw them, as he did not return to England after his marriage, but spent his holidays in the United States. I used to correspond with my sister-in-law though, and she told me a great deal about the children and their doings. The heat of the West Indies did not suit James, and he became very ill. The doctor said that the only thing to cure him was to go for a few years to an extremely cold climate. So he arranged with a Missionary Society to send him to work among the Indian tribes on the borders of

Alaska, in the far North West of Canada. It was a very wild place, quite unfit, so we thought, for a man to take a young family to live. His wife, however, was an adventurous woman, and she would neither let him go alone nor would she be parted from her children, so they all started off on their great adventure. We had one letter telling us about some of their thrilling experiences, then came sad news from the Missionary Society. They had all fallen victims to an epidemic of fever that was raging among the Indians, and the whole family was reported dead and buried.

" It was about eighteen months after this that we heard again from the headquarters of the Missionary Society at Vancouver. A strange thing had happened. An official in the Forestry Service of the Canadian Government had been inspecting the district near which James had been stationed, and among a tribe of Indians he had noticed a little white girl of perhaps six years old. He spoke to her in English and she evidently understood him, and tried to reply, but in such a broken and halting fashion that she must almost have forgotten her own language. He made inquiries about her, and found it extremely difficult to get any information. He could not talk the particular native dialect of the tribe, and he had not a good interpreter with him. All that the Indians could or would say was that they had found the child, and had saved her from perishing with cold and hunger. He was due to return immediately by a small steamer, before the river froze and became blocked with ice, so he had no time for any further inquiry. He insisted upon taking the little girl away with him. The Indians were most unwilling to let her go, they seemed to think her a kind of mascot, and said she brought luck to their hunting and fishing.

" As a government official, however, he used his authority, and took the child to Vancouver, to the missionary headquarters. It was naturally supposed that she must be one of James Barrett's family who had escaped the fever, though she spoke English so imperfectly and seemed so frightened when questioned that they could get nothing from her, not even her name. They had placed her temporarily in an orphanage at Vancouver, but they wished to know whether they should send her to her relations in England.

" Of course we telegraphed to them to send the child off as soon as a suitable escort could be found, and that we would meet her at Liverpool. In course of time you arrived, in charge of a Y.W.C.A. secretary, and you were handed over to us. I shall never forget our first sight of you, Jean! You were a little fair-haired, shrinking, timid creature of six or seven, with your arm in a sling, desperately frightened of strangers, and most unwilling to come with us. You clung to Mrs. Johnson and cried, and finally Uncle Charlie had to carry you off in his arms. We tried to comfort you in the train, and we got you home somehow, though it was a most agitating journey. You were so over-wrought and ill that we put you to bed and sent for a doctor. You only just escaped brain fever. For a fortnight I never left you day or night.

" When you had turned the corner and were beginning to get better, I had a long talk with the doctor. He said the terrible adventures, through which you must undoubtedly have passed in the forest, had overstrained your nervous system, and that, if we wished you to grow up a normal and healthy child, we must never refer to your former experiences, but just let you completely forget them, and make a fresh start.

" ' Don't ask her any questions or encourage her to

dwell upon her past,' he said; ' her future depends
upon putting her old life behind her.'

" Uncle Charlie and I were confronted with a big
problem now. Directly we saw you we were sure
that this little flaxen-haired creature could not be one
of James Barrett's children, who were all dark. Some
mistake had evidently been made, and you were not
our niece. We began very soon to get so fond of you,
though, that we decided we should like to keep you.
We had no children of our own, and you seemed just
to have fallen into our arms. Of course we wrote to
the Missionary Society at Vancouver, explaining the
situation, and they promised to cause inquiries to be
made about you among the Indians, but they never
heard anything from that source.

" After your illness we just let a curtain fall in your
mind between your old life and your new one. You
soon improved in health and you grew so merry and
cheerful you seemed a different child altogether. You
were quite ready to adopt us as Uncle and Auntie.
We named you our ' mascot ', because almost directly
after you came we sold several pictures, and got our
work accepted in the Academy and the Salon.

" It was a question what to call you. I suggested
Daisy, after the youngest of the James Barretts, but
your uncle didn't like Daisy. Then we made a discovery.
When you came to us you had on your arm a gold
bangle. I took it off when you were ill, and put it
away. On examining it again, we found that inside
there was engraved the word Jean. It must be
your name, and, at the risk of reviving a memory, we
ventured to use it. I thought you looked at me quickly
the first time I called you Jean, but you said nothing.

" Now, dear, this is all my part of the story and
explains yours a little, but even yet the two parts don't

fit together quite, and we don't know who you are. It doesn't matter, because you're just like a real niece to us. When we go back to the house I'll show you the bangle. I have it locked in my jewel box. I tried to keep all this from you, but you chanced to see the photo and the family record in the Bible, and I could tell you were wondering about it. Uncle Charlie and I talked it over, and decided that, if you asked, it would be better to let you know the history of your past life. You're twelve years old, and you're not nervous and frightened as you were at first. It can't do you any harm to revive old memories, so long as you don't let your mind dwell upon them. It's often wiser to bring a complex to the surface, and then just put it away and finish with it.

"Whoever you were you're our niece now, and we love you, and mean to do our best for you."

CHAPTER VI

Distinguished Foreigners

When Mrs. Barrett had finished her talk with Jean, and they had returned to the bungalow, she went to her bedroom, and unlocking a small leather jewel case, took out a little gold bangle. It seemed to be of Eastern workmanship and had a curious pattern chased upon it, of birds and flowers. Inside the name Jean could be deciphered quite plainly. Jean took it up and examined it carefully.

" Yes, I remember it," she said. " I used to wear it on my arm. The Indian children tried to steal it away from me, but their old granny would never let them. She said it was part of my luck, and that there would be bad hunting and fishing if ever they took it off. They were afraid of her, because she used to make charms over a smoky fire."

" The Indians must have thought you were a mascot. That's what Uncle Charlie and I called you when first you came to us."

" What exactly *is* a mascot? I thought it was one of those golliwogs or black cats that people fasten on their cars."

" It's a very old French superstition. Certain orphan children, who were foundlings, were considered to bring the greatest good fortune to those who adopted them and were kind to them. In Provence, if a child got a reputation for being a mascot, the farmers would almost quarrel which should have possession of it, because they thought their crops would prosper and their cows would give more milk while it was in their house. Funnily enough, they didn't think the child itself would have good luck—it would only bring luck to others. If it happened to walk into the village shop in the morning, the shopkeeper would be sure to have many customers that day, and if it made the sign of the cross on the fishing-boats they would have good catches."

" Have I brought luck to your painting?" twinkled Jean.

" It may be a coincidence, but it seems as if you have."

" You called Barney a mascot, too?"

" Well, Uncle Charlie's picture of him got into the Academy and was sold."

" It's rather nice to think of myself as a mascot," said Jean. " Perhaps the girls at school will do their work better when I'm there. If I don't know my own lessons I shall just feel ' well, never mind, I'm helping others to know theirs '!"

" *That's* not the way to look at it!" laughed Aunt Nora. " Mascots have to do their part in this workaday world just the same as other people, so don't flatter yourself you can walk through life in that fashion. No one will fasten you on the bonnet of his motor-car, I can assure you. Well, shall I lock the bangle up again?"

" May I keep it myself?" begged Jean. " Of course it's too small for me to wear now, but I feel as if I should like to have it. No, Auntie! You needn't be afraid that I'm going to be morbid or silly about it.

I got over nerves years ago, but it's the one and only thing I've brought from my queer past, and I've a great fancy to put it away in my treasure box. You don't mind? Oh, thanks!"

For a few days after this revelation of her former history, Jean was very quiet and absorbed. She could not help thinking about it and wondering who she really was. Mr. and Mrs. Barrett judged it best to bury the subject, and not speak of it again, but they were extra kind and affectionate, as if trying to show her that, if not blood-relations, they at any rate stood in the position of uncle and aunt to her. They were so cheery, and suggested so many happy little plans for the future, that she soon began to recover her usually buoyant spirits. After all, what did it matter? She loved them and was content to be their adopted niece. She even began to feel that it was rather romantic to have such a past. She was a dreamer, and liked to invent stories. Here was a mystery to which she might make up all sorts of possible or impossible solutions. Acting on a hint from Mrs. Barrett, she kept the matter to herself. There was no need for the world to know the exact circumstances of her relationship to them. She did not wish to go about labelled as a foundling.

Had they still been living at Monaco, she might have brooded far more, but the healthy influence of school distracted her mind and gave her plenty of other things to think about. Tennis had started. She left her racquet at Tresco House, and played there in all her spare time. Few of the other girls had had much practice, so she found she was considered to be doing well, and was regarded with favour by Enid and Sheila. With Vera too she began to form quite a friendship. They had taken to one another at first acquaintance. Vera was eager and enthusiastic, and selected Jean for a chum in preference to one of the boarders.

Both the girls liked Betty, but she could never stay after four o'clock, having to catch her motor-boat. Jean, on the contrary, would linger when afternoon school was over, and play tennis until the boarders were called in for tea. In this way she got to know some of them much better, and either revised or established her first impressions.

One day, after dinner, when it was too wet to play tennis, the elder girls collected in the schoolroom, watching the rain, and trying to think of ways to amuse themselves.

" I should think you wish you were back on the Riviera, Jean," said Betty.

" Well, it can rain there sometimes, and pretty hard too. On the whole, though, it's much finer than in England."

" I often wish I were back in Singapore," said Phyllis. " The water used to be really warm there when we bathed. We could stay in for hours."

" Any crocodiles?" inquired Peggie.

" Yes, plenty. There was a fence round the bathing pool to keep them out."

" We had the same in Africa," said Peggie calmly.

" In Africa? Didn't know you'd ever been there? Have you really?"

" Born there, my good child. You don't know everything, because I haven't confided my family history before. I was saving it up for my autobiography. Oh, yes, I'm going to write my autobiography soon, and put in all my thrilling adventures. Who'll promise to buy it when it's published?"

The girls giggled.

" Were you *really* born in Africa?" asked Phyllis, incredulously.

" Right in the wilds, near Timbuctoo," said Peggie, eyeing the circle defiantly. " My father was the British Commissioner out there—the great white chief, the natives used to call him. They came from hundreds of miles round to be judged. My father and the Emir of Boogoowalla were the two most important people. I remember the Emir very well."

" What was he like?"

" Black as coal, with teeth like ivory. He always grinned at me. He said if he ever came over to England he'd be sure to call and see me. I don't know whether he has a visiting card though!"

" She's making up," sneered Enid.

" Am I? Just wait till my book's published and you'll see."

" You're the biggest fibber I've ever met!" laughed Betty.

" I really *was* born in Africa," maintained Peggie.

Any further details of her previous career were cut short by Miss Horace, who came to remind her that she ought to be practising at the piano. She departed, making surreptitious grimaces behind the teacher's back.

The little circle of girls looked at one another.

" I think she's just showing off," said Enid.

" She likes to be in the limelight."

" Rather! I never believe half she tells me."

Peggie's extraordinary yarns only amused her schoolmates, but they keenly resented the rags that she often played upon them, and which were sometimes mixed with a spice of malice. When Enid found her tennis racquet in the lily pond there was trouble, and girls whose books were hidden or pencils misplaced made formal complaints.

One afternoon, Vera, Jean, and Betty had gone to the tennis court after dinner. Betty had brought some toffee to school, and as she had no pocket she put the paper bag down in a flower bed close to the seat, while the three of them joined Sheila in a game.

" Now for a little refreshment," said Betty, when the set was over.

She went to look for her paper bag, but it was nowhere to be seen. On the seat, however, sat Peggie, sucking something which made a large lump in her cheek. Betty looked at her suspiciously.

" What are you eating?" she asked.

" Toffee. Most delicious."

" Where did you get it?"

" The piskies left it for me among the flowers! Wasn't it kind of them?"

" Peggie White! You knew that toffee was mine."

" I knew nothing of the sort. Finding's keeping!"

" I call it stealing!"

" Do you? *I* don't."

" Then we've different codes of morals."

" Sorry, I'm sure. You shouldn't leave toffee lying about if you want to eat it yourself. My code is ' take what you can get and be thankful '."

Peggie's speech was incommoded by the large lump in her mouth. She got up and sauntered away, leaving three most indignant girls behind.

" She *is* the limit," said Vera.

" It was home-made toffee," regretted Betty. " Mrs. Hoskins made it as a surprise for me."

" And she's eaten it all."

" Greedy pig!"

" I should like to pay her out."

" She jolly well deserves a good rag played on *her*."

" So she does," said Betty thoughtfully. " It would serve her right. I say! I have an idea."

" What is it?"

" You must wait. I haven't quite evolved it yet."

" Oh, *do* tell us."

" No, I must think it out. Jean, are you coming to play tennis on Saturday afternoon?"

" Yes, I nearly always do."

" I'm staying the week-end at school because Grannie and Grandad will be in London," said Vera.

" Oh, good! And I'm spending the day with Iva. We're both coming for tennis. The boys are going to Cousin Frank's. It all fits in splendidly."

" How tantalizing you are! *What* fits in?"

" I shan't tell you. If I can engineer what I want it shall all be a magnificent surprise."

" Just one hint, please!"

" No. I can keep my own secrets."

Though Betty lived on Dinas Island she had relations at Port Erbyn, and sometimes stayed with her cousin Iva, a pretty little girl, younger than herself, who also attended Tresco House. Her brothers, Harry and Michael, went every day by train to school at Lestormel, in company with their cousins, Tom and Chris, with whom they occasionally spent a Saturday afternoon, as Mr. Frank Tregarthen, the father of Tom and Chris, had a small sailing yacht, and liked to take the four boys out with him.

On the following Saturday, the boarders and some of the day girls assembled at the tennis court for a practice. They were joined by Betty and Iva, who arrived looking much amused and evidently bursting with suppressed excitement.

" Where's Miss Horace?" asked Connie Chapman.

" She and Miss Suffolk have gone yachting this afternoon," replied Enid. " Mr. Frank Tregarthen offered to take them."

" In that dear little white yacht? I wish he'd take *me*! Where's Miss Mason?"

" Don't ask me," laughed Sheila. " I heard a hint that her fiancé was over at Port Erbyn to-day. It's her Saturday off in any case. She's possibly on the back of his motor-bike tearing along at fifty miles an hour."

" Then we're quite on our own?"

" Yes. Miss Suffolk said she was sure we didn't need a teacher with us the whole time. I'm to pour out tea if they're not back by five."

" Oh, come along then, let's arrange the sets."

For an hour the girls played tennis, and were sitting resting on the bank when Iva, who had disappeared, came hurrying back through the gate.

" There are some most extraordinary visitors in the garden," she explained. " Foreigners, and so queer! They're asking to see Miss Peggie White."

" *Me?*" exclaimed Peggie jumping up.

" Yes. They said something about knowing your father in Africa. It's certainly *you* they want."

" Where are they?"

" Close to the summer house. They're waiting there."

Peggie, looking much mystified, set off towards the garden.

" I vote we go too," suggested Betty, running after her.

The other girls got up and followed. Their curiosity was keenly aroused.

Certainly Iva had not exaggerated the queerness of the visitors who were standing near the summer house.

There were four of them, and their appearance suggested Africa. Their countenances were black as ebony; they were dressed in gorgeous striped garments, wore turbans on their heads, and sandals on their dusky feet. At the arrival of the party of girls, they prostrated themselves and bent their turbans to the earth in humble salutation. On rising once more, one of the number stepped forward.

"Me speak a leetle Eengleesh," he began. "We come to seek Mees Peggie White."

"I'm Miss Peggie White," replied that astonished schoolgirl.

The four once again prostrated themselves, almost grovelling before her. When their equilibrium was restored their spokesman continued his address:

"We come from the Emir of Boogoowalla. He in England now on visit to King George. He send greetings to daughter of Great White Chief. He like to have come himself—but had to attend audience of King and go to grand feast at Palace. He send us instead, and tell us say he beg you receive gifts from your humble slaves. He bring them from Boogoowalla for daughter of Great White Chief."

From the folds of their voluminous garments each of the visitors produced a bulky paper parcel. They laid these at Peggie's feet, and then retired to a respectful distance.

Peggie, much mystified, gazed from the parcels to the dusky faces of the ambassadors.

"How did you come?" she inquired.

"We come in special royal motor-car lent by His Gracious Majesty King George as act of kindness to his subject Emir of Boogoowalla. If daughter of Great White Chief accept gifts, we go back to London to tell Emir she receive them from her slaves."

"Oughtn't you to thank them?" whispered Betty, as Peggie began picking up the parcels.

"Yes. Please tell the Emir of Boogoowalla that I'm very grateful to him for his presents—but—I *should* like to know why it is that two of his subjects have blue eyes? And that one of them speaks English so very well?"

At this unexpected question, the embassy seemed prepared to depart in a hurry. Peggie, however, seized the hindmost by his burnous, and with a skilful and well directed grab removed his turban, revealing a crop of short fair hair.

"Boys! I knew it!" she said. "Now, what is the meaning of this rag? Who are you?"

Betty and Iva, having chased the other three, now brought them back and presented them.

"You'd better introduce yourselves," said Betty.

The four, standing in a grinning row, took their own roll-call.

"Kaganda—chief of the Busaka tribe—otherwise Tom Tregarthen."

"Machako—chief of the Kavirondo tribe—Chris Tregarthen—at your service, madam!"

"Luba—chief of the Busoga in Africa—but Harry Tregarthen in England."

"Mengo—chief of the Kikewollygoogoos—but I'm Michael Tregarthen at home."

"You're sports at any rate," commented Peggie.

"Don't you want to open our offerings?" asked Chris.

"No, I don't. I can guess what's inside them. Pieces of coal, I expect. Where did you get those topping costumes?"

"From Aunt Selina," laughed Tom.

"I wonder what you'd look like if you washed your faces?"

The other girls had now crowded round and were examining the dresses and the make-up of the pseudo African chiefs.

"There's a basin of water and some soap and a towel in the summer house," suggested Betty. "You'd better wash yourselves and take those things off and go home. If Miss Suffolk and Miss Horace were to come back they might see the joke, but, on the other hand, they might not."

"They won't be back yet awhile. I told Dad to take them a good sail and keep them out even if they were sea-sick!" replied Tom.

"Then you knew about it, Betty?"

"And you too, Iva?"

"I believe you planned it all."

"Just like you."

"Rather a good rag, though."

"I was taken in for a minute or two myself."

"They did it so well."

"I could see a bit of white skin under one of the turbans when they bumped their heads on the ground."

The girls' eager comments showed that they had enjoyed the fun, and even Enid was laughing.

"Hurry off those bad brothers and cousins of yours, Betty," she said. "Tell them to take their parcels with them. Doesn't anybody want to go back to the tennis court? We've time for another set before tea. Leave those mummers to wash their faces, and come along."

"Were you really born at Boogoowalla, Peggie?" asked Connie, as they walked away.

"If you want to know my birthplace, consult *Who's Who*," answered Peggie loftily. "You'll find me among the list of the Peerage, with a description of my distinguished ancestry. My sports, recreations, hobbies, country seat, telephone number, and number of motor-car."

"Was Peggie really taken in at first?" whispered Jean to Vera. "She looked so astonished."

"I think she's played too many rags herself to be easily gulled. But she's over-reached herself for once. She wouldn't open the parcels, and there was some toffee inside each. Betty told me so. The boys are eating it themselves in the summer house! Peggie will be wild when she hears what she's missed."

CHAPTER VII

Vera comes to Tea

Jean was not very quick in forming new friendships, but she was getting to know and like some of the girls at Tresco House, especially Vera, who had " taken her up " from the first. Vera was fond of painting, and would often ask her about the artists she had met in France, and the picture galleries she had visited in Italy.

There was nothing about which Jean more enjoyed talking, of course.

" Your uncle and aunt must be very clever to get into the Royal Academy and the Salon," she commented one day. " I wish I could see some of their pictures."

" I wish you could," replied Jean. " They have some jolly sketches that they did last winter at Monaco. I wonder how we could manage it? Do you think Miss Suffolk would let you come to tea—'specially if Aunt Nora wrote a proper formal invitation?"

" Oh, how jolly! I believe she would if she telephoned first to ask Grannie. I'd adore to come and look at everything."

" Well, I'll ask Aunt Nora, and see if we can wangle it."

" Yes, do. And then perhaps Grannie would let me ask you to come home with me some time for the

week-end. Then I could show you all *my* belongings—
my dog Tim, and my white Persian cat, and the three
kittens. By the by, how would you like a kitten to
keep? We can't keep them all, and we want to give
two of them away."

Jean shook her head regretfully.

" I'd *like* one, but Aunt Nora won't have a cat.
We've only got the bungalow till the autumn, and if
we had a kitten what should we do with it when we
went away? It's difficult enough to take Barney. We
had to leave him in quarantine at Dover when we
arrived in England."

" Do you expect to be going abroad again next
winter then?"

" I don't know. It depends where Uncle Charlie
wants to paint. He likes Port Erbyn for the present,
but perhaps he'll have sketched all the best subjects
by autumn and be glad of a change. The weather is
so much better in France and Italy during the winter.
It's quite possible to sit out and sketch there, when
it's freezing or pouring in England."

" And what about you? Will they take you with
them, or leave you here as a boarder?"

" Take me with them, I hope!"

" Should you go to a foreign school then? That
would be rather sport!"

" No. I've always done a few lessons with Aunt
Nora before."

" Wouldn't you like to be a boarder here next
winter? Betty will be coming in October, when it
gets too stormy for them to use their motor-boat
every day. If we three were all together we'd have
such fun!"

" It sounds jolly—but—I don't know!"

" Think it over, and just suggest it some time to

your uncle and aunt. Perhaps they'd like the idea. It would be scrummy!"

Jean was not at all sure that Uncle Charlie and Aunt Nora would entertain such a project or that she wished to suggest it to them. She loved their wandering life abroad, and even the company of Betty and Vera did not seem to offer enough compensation for spending a winter at school in England.

She asked if she might have Vera to tea, and Mrs. Barrett readily agreed.

"Have her by all means. Yes, Thursday will do very well if she can come then. You can bring her back with you at four o'clock."

"May we have Cornish cream for tea? And cakes? Say yes, like a darling!"

"Certainly. I'll bake you one of those French cakes you're so fond of. Madame Rompier gave me her recipe."

"Oh, that would be jolly. And some little cakes as well?"

"I'll do my best for you."

"Thanks immensely!"

The invitation was duly given, and Miss Suffolk rang up Mrs. Anderson, who gave the required permission.

"I may go home with you at four," rejoiced Vera. "And Miss Horace says she'll walk up and fetch me back about half-past six, so that I can do my prep from seven to eight. I suggested I should take my books and do it with you, but she wouldn't hear of that! She said we should just be talking all the time instead of working."

"Well, I'm glad you can come! We ought to have a marvellous time."

Jean told her aunt that the invitation was accepted,

and she promised to try and find the recipe for the cake, which was somewhere among her papers in her desk.

"I hope it will bake all right in this kind of oven," she said.

"The one you made at Monaco was lovely, Auntie. I'm sure Vera will like it."

On Thursday morning an unfortunate thing happened. Freda, the maid, forgot to wind her alarum clock and overslept herself. Jean woke late, looked at her watch, and hurried up to rouse Freda, snatched what she could from the larder and set off for school. Mr. and Mrs. Barrett, who were used to foreign ways, generally had their morning coffee brought to their bedroom, and they were not yet awake.

"Shall I knock at their door and remind Auntie about that cake?" thought Jean, as she was leaving the bungalow. "Oh, she can't forget surely, and I'm so late I shall only just be in time if I run half the way. It will be all right!"

It was an unlucky day for Jean at school, one of those days when everything seems to go wrong. She accidentally trod on Sheila's stilo pen, which had fallen to the floor, and broke it, and was called a "clumsy idiot" by its indignant owner. She found that in her haste to rush to school she had lost her handkerchief. Of course Miss Horace asked her the only questions in the history lesson which she did not know, and put the questions which she could have answered to other members of the form. In the hurry of leaving home that morning she had forgotten to put her French exercise in her bag, and was ordered to stay in the schoolroom after dinner and write it again. She made several stupid blunders in the French class. Madame Héger stared at her and said she was not attending, and that there was no excuse for her, as having lived in France she ought to know better than to make such mistakes. Jean sighed and wondered what was boding next in the way of ill-luck. She comforted herself, however, with the prospect of Vera coming to tea. That, at any rate, was something to which she might look forward with pleasure.

The day dragged along somehow, as even the worst days will, and four o'clock came at last. Books were put away, home lessons collected, desks closed, and school dismissed. Five minutes afterwards Jean and Vera were walking along the road towards the bungalow. They found plenty to talk about on the way. Vera liked to chatter and always had much to say about everything.

They reached the gate in course of time and went in at the front door. Jean took her friend into the sitting-room, where she expected to see her aunt. No one was there, however, and the tea table was not laid. Asking Vera to wait a minute, she hurried into the studio. That also was empty. She ran into the kitchen to find Freda. That also was unoccupied, and a large bucket of soot stood by the unlighted stove. With a terrible sinking at heart Jean fled through the back door to see if the missing family were in the garden. Hearing the gate swing, she turned down the path, and was greeted tumultuously by Barney. Freda, carrying a pail of water in each hand, was coming towards the house.

"Oh, Freda!" cried Jean. "Is nothing ready? Where are Auntie and Uncle?"

Freda put down the buckets, and wiped a hot smutty face with a sooty apron.

"They're out painting. They went about twelve o'clock, and took some sandwiches and two thermos flasks with them."

"When will they be back?" gasped Jean. "Did they tell you?"

"I couldn't say, I'm sure. Mrs. Barrett said we could have a cold supper to-night, and I might as well clean out the kitchen stove. A job it's been too! That pipe was all blocked with soot."

"But, Freda, I've brought a friend back to tea! Did Auntie forget?"

"She didn't say anything to me about your bringing a friend."

"Oh, what *am* I to do? There's no tea ready and the stove out! Did Auntie make a cake and get some cream?"

Freda shook her head and began to take up the pails.

"Well, look here, we *must* have some tea somehow," continued poor Jean. "Put the kettle on the spirit lamp, and I'll lay the table while you're cutting the bread and butter. Be as quick as you can, won't you? I'm sure you're a sport?"

Freda retreated rather sulkily to the kitchen. In her own way she felt as aggrieved as Jean. She did not hurry overmuch. They might wait a little for their tea: if people would bring back visitors on a day when the stove was being cleaned they couldn't expect busy folks to be at their beck and call.

Making what apology she could to Vera, Jean laid the table, found a pot of jam, the remains of yesterday's cake and some biscuits, and after a tiresome wait the kettle boiled, and she filled the teapot. It was a poor spread in comparison with the dainty tea she had intended to give her guest, and she felt very crestfallen.

"Aren't your uncle and aunt coming in?" asked Vera.

"They'll be in soon, I hope, but we'd better not wait for them," answered Jean mendaciously. As they had evidently forgotten she was bringing a visitor, they might quite possibly be out until seven or eight o'clock, if they were interested in the subjects they were painting. She knew their Bohemian ways only too well.

She acted hostess to the best of her ability, and tried to talk brightly, but all the time she felt things were falling rather flat.

" I should like to see the pictures," said Vera, when tea was over.

" We'll go into the studio. I'm sorry Uncle's out, but *I* can show them to you."

Here matters went better. Vera was really interested in the numerous canvases which Jean placed in turn on the big easel, and admired picturesque corners of Monaco, peeps of the Mediterranean, fishing-boats at St. Tropez, and street scenes in Toulon.

" I think they're very clever. How I wish I could paint! Do you ever sketch?"

" Sometimes. I've done a few little bits, but of course they aren't any good."

" Oh, do show me! Where are they?"

" They're in my bedroom."

" Let me see them."

" All right! Come along to my room."

Jean had dabbled in art under her uncle's instructions, and if not really talented, had produced some quite creditable sketches, which she had fastened with drawing-pins to the walls of her bedroom. Vera thought them worthy of high praise.

" I only wish *I* could paint like that," she said. " Haven't you anything else to show me? You told me you had some foreign curios."

" They're not much. Just little things I had given me in Rome and Venice," replied Jean, opening a box and exhibiting an Etruscan lamp, some Venetian beads, a cut-glass scent bottle, a stamped leather purse, a silver bonbonnière, and other trifles, and explaining what they were.

"What's this?" asked Vera suddenly, snatching up the precious gold bangle that lay among the other treasures.

"That! Oh, I used to wear it always when I was a little girl. It's too small for me now. Look! It has 'Jean' inside it."

Vera turned the bangle over and over with the greatest curiosity.

"Who gave it to you?" she asked.

"My father and mother, I suppose, but I don't remember."

"Are they both dead?"

"Yes."

"Where did you live when they were alive?"

"In the north of Canada."

"Can you remember them?"

"Not very well—you see, I was so young, and—and—I was lost—or stolen—and lived among the Indians for a while."

"You lived among the Indians!"

"Yes, until somebody found me."

"What do you mean? Oh, *do* tell me!"

Jean hesitated. She had not intended to say so much. It had just slipped out. Vera was looking at her with deep interest.

"*Do* go on and tell me," she urged.

It was perhaps unwise, but Jean was anxious to conciliate her friend to make up for the lack of hospitality that had been offered her, and in an impulsive moment she began to pour out the events of her childhood. Vera listened with wide-open eyes.